AGENTS OF CHANGE

AGENTS OF CHANGE

A MENOPAUSAL SUPERHEROES COLLECTION

SAMANTHA BRYANT

Charlotte, NC

FALSTAFF
BOOKS

WWW.FALSTAFFBOOKS.COM

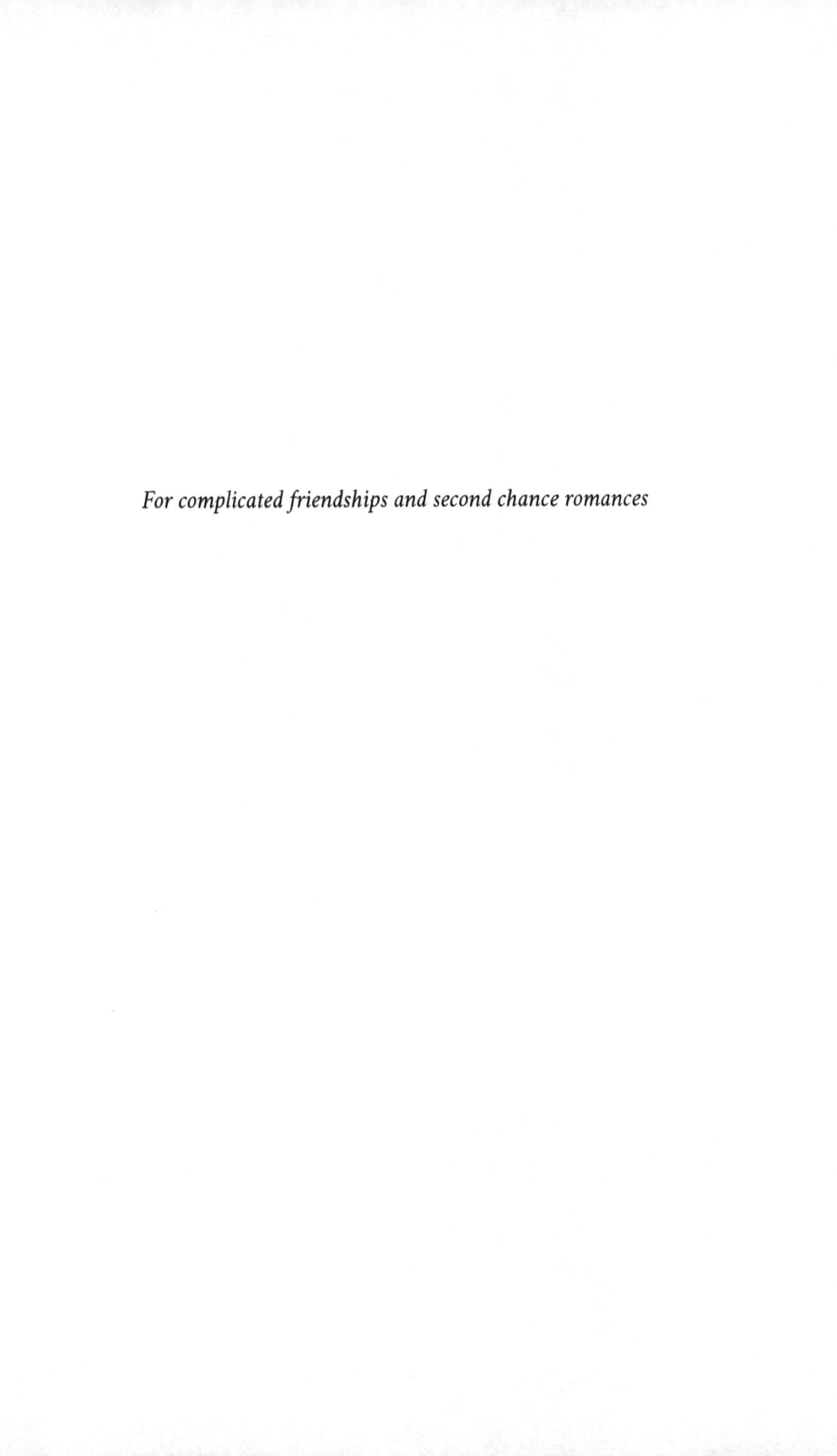

For complicated friendships and second chance romances

I

THE GOOD WILL TOUR

JESSICA AND LEONEL: A GOOD DISTRACTION

J essica Roark checked again to make sure none of her blond hair stuck out of the red Flygirl wig she wore to disguise her identity. She tugged her top down so it would lie smoothly over her hips, then pulled it back up because it showed too much cleavage. The blue and white public appearance version of her costume wasn't skimpy, but the flattering design lacked the seamless functionality of the all-black work clothes she wore when she expected to fight. The show clothes weighed less without the Kevlar, weaponry and communications gear, but somehow that made it less comfortable.

Maybe Walter could talk to the wardrobe people. He could make a science-based argument about wind resistance or something and they'd listen. There were perks in having a boyfriend with pull.

She verified her mask placement again and touched the secret pocket sewn into the built-in sports bra where she kept the supply of emeralds granting her full control over her flight. When she pulled out her compact and a lipstick for a third time, Leonel reached over and took it from her, tucking it back into the gym bag under the sink. "You are perfect. Stop fussing."

Jessica grabbed her best friend's hand and smiled up into his handsome face. "I'm so glad you came with me."

Leonel's discomfort with the limelight dwarfed her own, but he returned her smile. He avoided meet-and-greets and other public appearances as much as he could. Except for this one. This time, he'd volunteered. "I wouldn't miss it! I know this is special to you."

This one was special. Springfield Women's Hospital had saved her life. Lending her star power to a fundraiser seemed very little to ask in return. Of course, the hospital didn't know Flygirl had once been a patient here.

It had been a strange year. Ever since the Department had gone public, revealing the existence of people like her, her life had gone from complicated to bizarre in short order. Now, she and the other "Freaks" took on cases beyond the understanding of regular law enforcement, the kind needing special abilities to keep people safe or where special abilities caused the problem.

It was weird living in a world where she fought people who could turn invisible or move lightning fast, where the story aired on the six o'clock news alongside coverage of celebrity appearances and new laws proposed in Congress. Two years ago, all this would have been Internet rumors based on fuzzy cell phone camera pictures.

Two days ago, Ellen herself had interviewed Jessica on her national talk show and wanted to know what it really felt like to fly. Jessica had told her to imagine the moment at the top of the roller coaster, right before you drop, the bubbly feeling in the belly where excitement intermixed with panic. That was the closest thing to flying she had ever experienced before she and gravity had renegotiated their contract.

When the Director had approached her about being the public face for the Unusual Cases Unit, the openly acknowledged part of the Department, she'd been flattered. Anxious to repay what she saw as considerable debt for her medical care, technology and new skills, she'd agreed.

But the idea and reality were quite different. Seeing her own face on television, even disguised by the light blue mask, was always jarring. She had never sought fame, and the attention was disconcerting, to say the least.

But Jessica believed in the work and liked making a difference. These public appearance events were an important part of that, too—maybe as important as catching criminals. In a way, she'd trained for this all her life. Back when she had been Mrs. Corporate Elite, she'd worn fancy dresses to charity balls. Before her battle with cancer, early menopause, and the unexpected side effects of drinking an herbal tea. She liked the costume and causes better now.

Springfield Women's Hospital treated Jessica before she had superpowers, though no one knew Flygirl and Jessica Roark were the same person. The staff had seen her through her oophorectomy and the follow-up treatment with kindness and patience.

She'd been lucky, well–insured, and able to handle the bills. Other women deserved the same standard of care. So when the Director asked her to visit patients and attend a fundraiser as part of a Good Will Tour, she had not hesitated. She wasn't sure why she felt so nervous now, other than she wanted it go well.

"They're going to love you." Leonel said again, resting a well-manicured hand on her shoulder. His fastidiousness over small details charmed her. She wondered what he'd been like before Dr. Liu's products had changed everything. Had he been a devotee of beauty salons and spas like her mother?

Until his forty-eighth year, Leonel had been a short, curvy Hispanic woman, a mother and grandmother named Linda Alvarez. Then, one fateful shower had given him strength, stature, and a penis, thanks to some mysterious interaction between his own body chemistry and Dr. Liu's soap. Leonel's loving heart had never changed, though his body had. She was so glad he had opted to come with her today. Having him along would make this easier.

Jessica straightened a piece of Leonel's hair bunched up under his mask. "If they don't, maybe you can pick up a desk or something and distract them with your muscles."

Leonel flexed ostentatiously and did the worst imitation of Arnold

Schwarzenegger the world had ever heard. "Hasta la vista, baby." When he winked, they both laughed.

Jessica gave herself one last pat down and turned to the door. "Okay, I'm as ready as I'll ever be. Let's go."

J essica knew the layout of the hospital quite well from all the time she'd spent there as a patient but let the woman from the publicity department lead the way. Even here, in the office areas, the acrid hospital smell brought up memories that made Jessica's guts churn. She couldn't help but turn her head to peer down the hall leading to the chemotherapy rooms. She rubbed her arm, remembering the soreness that had accompanied all the needles. They wouldn't be going back there today, thankfully.

Their first stop on the Good Will Tour was the atrium, a glass and steel area at the front of the hospital where patients and families waited for treatment and news. Their guide paused in the doorway, making sure the cameras were ready, then led the two into the center of the room. "Ladies and gentlemen, we have some special visitors with us today at Springfield Women's Hospital. Please welcome Fuerte and Flygirl!"

Taking her cue, Jessica rose into the air, careful not to fly too high as she flexed into a heroic pose that always made her sons smile. It wouldn't do to get tangled in the light fixtures. Using her powers indoors required more care.

The room went silent for a beat or two, then Jessica lowered herself to the floor, twirling in gentle circles as she did. Someone said, "Wow!" in a soft burst of amazement and admiration.

After that, cheerful chatter filled the room and Jessica and Leonel walked around shaking hands and signing autographs. Posing for a photograph with two young women wearing colorful scarfs over their bald heads, Jessica's nerves fell away, grateful her presence could distract from the struggle for a few minutes.

She looked over to catch Leonel's eye and found him kneeling on the floor with four small children dangling from his extended arms. He stood slowly and the children giggled and squealed as their feet got further away from the tile floor. Mothers and grandmothers gazed on approvingly, both for his physique and for entertaining the kids.

Jessica's own boys worshipped "Tío Leonel" and this particular stunt never failed to elicit peals of laughter, especially from her oldest who had grown "too big" for most adults to hold him like that anymore. Having seen Leonel with his own grandchildren, she knew the affectionate playfulness came from a genuine delight in the happiness of children. When they spent an afternoon making deliveries for a food bank last winter, Leonel had wanted to take all the children home and make cookies.

Now that they'd done a few public events together, there was no denying his crowd appeal even if the attention made him uncomfortable. She had the showy power, but he had the charisma. She felt stiff and fake in comparison.

Leonel lowered the kids to the ground again, catching the one that almost toppled over and seating her on his knee. He gave them each a comic book featuring a cartoon version of himself as Fuerte titled *Leer es Poder*. Flipping the book upside down, you could peruse *Reading is Power* in English, too. Leonel thought his comic book persona a little over muscled, but Jessica thought it a very good likeness.

After the photo op people signaled their satisfaction and the woman from publicity waved the two heroes toward the exit.

Jessica swooped over to Leonel and looped her arm into his, levitating six inches off the floor to put her head level with his. She smiled at the crowd of children and parents gathered around his feet. "I'm afraid Fuerte and I have to move on now."

Leonel looked genuinely regretful. "Remember, *niños*, everyone has a battle to fight. I wish you the strength to fight yours." He blew them kisses and turned around, Jessica letting go to twirl beside him.

They left to the sound of applause and chatter. Jessica wondered how long it would take for a malaise of waiting and uncertainty to fall back over the room. She remembered the weariness of it very well.

E nsconced in a small office to wait for the return of their guide, Leonel reached for a bottle of water and sighed. "I wasn't sure about that line, but our Suzie knows her stuff."

Jessica had to agree. Suzie Grayson really understood the importance of public perception and had proven a master at manipulating it, without losing sight of the larger mission.

Leonel reached out and patted Jessica's fingers. "How are you doing? Is it too weird, being here?" he asked.

"I am fine," she assured him, and it was mostly true. No one here knew her as a survivor, like no one here knew Flygirl as Jessica Roark. Secrecy was important to her safety and that of her family, though it kept her at a distance from people sometimes. "I'm glad we could distract them for a bit," she added.

"Me too."

2

EVELYN TAKES MATTERS INTO HER OWN HANDS

E velyn Mueller was desperate.

Jeannie was dying.

That special study had been their last hope, and the hospital people turned them down. Jeannie didn't qualify, they said, as if denying a bank loan or a scholarship application, like refusing her wasn't signing her death certificate. They had to know she didn't have some other path to recovery. Evelyn could hardly believe the researchers could be so cold and cavalier.

Truth be told, Evelyn didn't understand the experimental process or what it entailed, but it didn't matter. If there was any chance at all it would save her wife, she wanted Jeannie to have it. Anything less amounted to murder. These people would let Jeannie die if Evelyn didn't do something.

The benefits counselor had said Jeannie couldn't tolerate the treatments, but Evelyn couldn't tolerate losing the love of her life. How could the treatments be worse than the disease hollowing Jeannie out?

Evelyn walked out when the woman brought out the brochure about hospice care. There had to be more they could do for her than "pain management" and "keeping her comfortable." This couldn't be the end. Not yet. They still had so many plans. They'd never made it to New Zealand like they always said they would. Twenty years together did not nearly equal the lifetime they had promised each other.

Today, she'd force them to change their minds.

———

The day she stumbled onto the information about the First Lady and hatched this plan, Evelyn been giving a tour at the capitol building. Her role on the governor's administrative staff included giving tours of the capitol building. Her group had been another AARP chapter bussed in from a rural part of the state to see the sights, meet their representatives, and, if they were lucky, shake the governor's hand.

Evelyn always got the retirees. She didn't mind. They could be pretty funny, blurting out thoughts that younger, more politic tourists would keep under wraps. Some people's filters wore out as they aged. Once, a man in her tour group had walked up to a portrait of the first governor and spit on the ground. He'd unzipped his fly and had prepared to show his displeasure with other bodily fluids when the security guards hauled him away.

That day's group had been pretty manageable. One lady insisted on touching her hair and one creepy old guy commented about how her skin color reminded him of a fine piece of chocolate, but no one had wandered off and caused a silver alert.

After the last tourist returned to her bus, Evelyn sat waiting for Miss Breeze to finish her phone call. She needed to turn in the headsets and microphone she used to help the elderly tourists hear her in the echoing halls before she could check out for the day. Only the office manager had the key to that closet.

While she waited, trying to discreetly flex her feet inside the dressy pumps she should never have worn to work on a day with so much walking, her gaze wandered the serene landscapes of state parks and landmarks hanging on the walls and Evelyn tried not to seem like she was eavesdropping.

She was, of course.

Miss Breeze would never gossip about the governor and his family, but she wasn't careful about what she left lying on her desk and paid little mind to her surroundings when focused on a call. Spending time in the inner offices, you could learn a lot about the governor's personal life.

Over the years, Evelyn had learned about the governor's peccadillos and indiscretions. She, and everyone else in the office, knew all about the first son's trips through rehab and the first daughter's ill-advised romances. Miss Breeze's phone chats provided more information than the governor's own newsletter.

The week before, waiting to sign her payroll sheet, Evelyn found out the governor's wife had been diagnosed with ovarian cancer and the prognosis wasn't good. She felt bad. She'd only met the First Lady a few times, but the woman had always been friendly and gracious. Evelyn appreciated how she'd worked to promote acceptance for a broader definition of marriage in their state. It gave her hope for the future. It allowed her to finally call Jeannie her wife and have the word mean something in the eyes of the law.

After holding up a finger to ask Evelyn to wait, Miss Breeze turned back to her call. "Yes, ma'am, thank you...Oh, good! Governor Cafry will be so pleased you could get his wife into the program..."

Evelyn suddenly felt weak. It was good she was already sitting down or she might have wavered on her feet. She watched discreetly, reading upside down as the woman wrote down "Cancer. Women's Hospital," a phone number, and a name.

"He'll call as soon as he gets back to the office. He and his wife have been praying for this opportunity. Thank you!"

Afterwards, Evelyn pretended she had not heard a thing as the office manager counted the headsets, checked them back in, and set them aside for sanitization before the next day's tour. Evelyn wandered out in a bit of a fog, only remembering she'd never gone back to her office to finish her paperwork and log out of her computer when she got halfway home.

A voice chanted in the back of her head.

It wasn't fair. It wasn't fair. *It wasn't fair.*

The voice was right.

It *wasn't* fair.

But Evelyn could make it fair.

E velyn arrived at the hospital mid-morning. Snooping around the office, she'd discovered the state's First Lady had been admitted in the wee hours of the morning to avoid attracting the attention of the press. By now, she would be settled into a private room, probably with a bouquet of daffodils and tulips, her favorite. The administrative staff knew from all the apology bouquets they'd ordered over the years.

Yes, she'd be there. All Evelyn had to do was get to her. Then, she'd have some leverage.

Wearing a hat and glasses, Evelyn didn't want to be readily identified. After her meltdown in the benefits office and her temper tantrum in the lobby, security would be keeping an eye out for her. They'd made a point of warning her that visitation could be blocked if she couldn't control herself. Jeannie wouldn't want that.

She couldn't afford to be stopped today; she needed to get inside. Once Evelyn held the governor's wife's life in her hands, she could make them save Jeannie.

It turned out she could have worn a bikini and rainbow clown wig and no one would have noticed her, not with Flygirl and Fuerte holding court in the lobby. It must have been part of the Good Will Tour the new Unusual Cases Unit sent around, trying to make the public a little less frightened by the idea of people who could fly and shoot lasers or whatever else they could do.

Evelyn had been too occupied with Jeannie's illness to spend much time considering whether these people were heroes or dangers to society, but that didn't mean she was completely unaware of the controversy surrounding them. The entire idea met a mixture of enthusiasm and trepidation, sometimes wrapped up together.

The Freaks, as most people called the UCU, were something between soldiers and superheroes, so far as Evelyn could tell. They wore masks when they worked, which didn't help with the trust factor, but they had been at the forefront of several high-profile news stories.

The Lizard Woman of Springfield, a character Evelyn had assumed akin to Bigfoot—fun, but fictional—now regularly appeared on the evening news. Evelyn had seen the footage of the fire-fight on campus last spring—the one with literal fire some woman could produce from her hands. The college had been left smoking and trampled. Did these so-called heroes make it better or worse?

Evelyn, along with everyone else across the country, had been forced to revise her beliefs about what was possible in a world that had seen a rise in seemingly impossible things. What scared her most was the idea that there were more of these people everywhere, and some would choose to harm, and conventional law enforcement wasn't equipped to deal with that. Even in the news broadcasts, when the UCU arrived on the scene, you could see the fear mixed with relief on the faces of more ordinary folk.

Unless one of them became a walking cure for cancer and could save Jeannie's life, they didn't matter to Evelyn. Barring the appearance of Chemo-Man or Stem-cellia, superheroes were useless.

Still, if people like this existed, better they served on the side of the law, even if the idea of super-powered police terrified her, too. The costumes and masks didn't alleviate her fears. They put her in mind of little kids playing dress up.

Right now, Evelyn couldn't have been more pleased with their presence, though. While everyone focused on the costumed spectacle, she skirted the crowd, walked past the deserted information desk and gift shop and stepped onto an elevator, a path she'd traveled far too many times in the past few months. The security guy hadn't pulled his eyes away from the red-haired woman twirling in her blue and white circus outfit. She couldn't have planned a better distraction.

In the elevator, she clicked the button for the fourth floor oncology ward, closed her eyes and let her head fall back against the cool metal wall. Her curls pushed forward around her face like a cloud. She'd spent a lot of time praying in this metal box, promising a God she only kind of believed in anything he wanted if only he'd find a way to save Jeannie. She'd gotten no answer, in words or in actions.

It was time to take matters into her own hands.

3

JESSICA AND LEONEL: WHAT MAKES A MOTHER

T he next part of the tour was harder: individual visits to the patients, the ones staying at the hospital, short or long term. Jessica remembered the random visitors from her own time as a patient with a mixture of gratitude and irritation.

She'd been touched to know people cared, and sometimes the distraction had brought her back from despair. But it was also difficult to find the energy to be kind and gracious, especially if the day had already been hard. What any one person in treatment needed and wanted at any given time was so individual, Jessica felt pushy in her garish blue and white tights. Luckily, Leonel was with her.

Before they entered the first room, he knocked softly on the door frame and leaned his head in. "You up for some visitors?"

The woman in the bed raised an arm and waved them in.

Despite his bright red shirt and sunshine yellow mask, Leonel managed to seem small and quiet as he tiptoed into the room. He sat primly in the chair beside the bed, his hands folded in his lap and smiled. "I am Fuerte and this is Flygirl."

"I know. They told us you'd be coming. I'm Ginny." The woman sounded tired but interested.

Leonel stood and padded quietly to the foot of the bed and the bulletin board with pictures and cards clipped to it. "May I?"

The woman nodded and Leonel unclipped a photograph of a woman sitting under a beach umbrella surrounded by a group of girls. He handed the photograph to the woman and her fingers brushed it gently. "Are these your girls? I have three daughters myself." He reached for his wallet and then let his hand drop. Showing people pictures of his family probably wasn't wise even if there had been a back pocket in his uniform, let alone a wallet inside it.

The woman ignored him and turned to Jessica. "Do you have children?"

"I do. Two boys." At their mention, Frankie and Max's faces sprang to mind. A wave of grief smacked her down with the weight of how it might have turned out. If she had not won her fight against cancer and her boys had grown up without her, as she'd feared. "They made this easier and harder," she gestured at the hospital walls.

"You're a survivor?" The woman's gaze sharpened and she pulled herself up to something nearer a sitting position.

"I am. Ovarian cancer. I'm two and a half years out." That piece of her history leaped out of her mouth before she could think about it. Seeing the hope that flashed in the woman's eyes, she couldn't regret saying it.

"How old are your boys?" the woman asked.

They spent the next few minutes talking about children, childbirth, and, to a lesser extent, Leonel's grandchildren. Ginny's daughters, they learned, all attended college—a senior, a junior, and a freshman. Luckily the tuition payments had already been made before their mother's diagnosis. Ginny was determined they would all graduate. "No matter what happens to me."

Between rooms, Leonel leaned against the wall. Jessica patted his arm. "It's hard, isn't it? Watching all these women in pain, fighting so hard."

"It makes me miss being a woman."

Jessica leaned back to look into her friend's face and saw he was serious. Confused, she blurted, "What difference does that make?"

"I'm a toucher. I want to hug these women, take their hands, squeeze their shoulders. But it's so different now that I'm like this." He spread out his arms, and Jessica noted the breadth of his biceps and the wide expanse of his chest, not without admiration. "I don't know how to offer comfort as a man," he said.

"But you are a comfort. When I need to talk, there's no one I would rather talk to. You listen like no one else."

"David doesn't think so. He says it is different now, though he still loves me. I feel like I haven't changed. Under my skin, I am the same person he married, but it makes a difference in how he sees me, how he talks to me, in what he thinks when I react. It's a very different matter, now, when I cry."

He lowered his voice. "I think it's different for these women, too. They are on guard with me in a way they aren't with you." He pointed back at the room they had left. "When we talked about our children, you were able to talk to her as a mother. I am a mother, too, but my experience is not counted the same because I wear a man's face. She wouldn't believe I'd ever been someone's mother, that I know what it is to carry a child within my body, and nurse her."

His sadness touched Jessica. It made her stop and consider things she might have said or done, hurting him unintentionally. "I didn't know you when you were a woman, Leonel." In fact, it was strange to consider that this tall, handsome man had ever been anything else, that, inside he still thought of himself as a woman.

He had told her that, sometimes, looking in the mirror was so startling that he jumped at the sight of his own face, even with three years to adjust to the transformation. Jessica's own changes had been quite an adjustment, especially before she found the emeralds that helped her control her flight, but she had never felt like she wasn't herself. In fact, sometimes she felt like she hadn't really been herself before, that her powers allowed a truer self to shine through.

Leonel ran a hand over his hair, then automatically smoothed it into place. "There are things I like about being a man. Things like my new voice and the ease of finding clothes, how cheap my haircuts are." The words were light, but the tone serious. "Also knowing my opinion will be listened to in a meeting and feeling safe walking alone at night. But there are times when I feel like it's in my way. Places I can't go anymore, or if I do, it won't be the same."

Jessica thought back to the time she and Leonel had gone to one of his favorite *peluquería* to get him a haircut, when his woman's haircut sat oddly against the new planes of his face. She remembered it as a great day, a fun time with her gay boyfriend.

But now that she knew Leonel better, she understood he had been performing for her, the manicurists, and the hair stylists, flirting to get past the awkwardness of being there and suddenly the center of attention in a woman's space. "Do you wish you could go back? To the way you were before?"

"Not really." Leonel seemed to mean it despite the wistfulness in his tone. "My life is exciting. Purposeful. I can make a difference in a larger way. I can literally save lives. This hero stuff...it's different than anything I knew as a woman, and part of me loves it. It would be hard to go back to my old life, even if I could. Maybe though, if I were able to keep the strength...But your Walter seems to think the two are intertwined."

Jessica floated off the floor to rest her arm across Leonel's shoulders. "Just keep being you, Leonel, whoever that is today."

Jessica found herself watching Leonel in the next few rooms, noticing the ways women reacted to his presence. He kept good humor when people said things like "Oh, you know how men are." He flirted gamely when that seemed to be what they wanted, though it made him uncomfortable. She saw the small flinches when people asked about his wife and the deflections he used to avoid assigning gender in the conversation, little things she'd never noticed before, like always saying "we" to avoid "husband" or "partner."

"I've been married for more than twenty years."

"Our children say…"

"D is so good with the grandchildren. Spoils them rotten."

By the time they finished with the room visits, both heroes were emotionally exhausted. "Almost done," Jessica said cheerfully. "Just lunch with the bigwigs, then we can get back to the easy stuff, like fighting crime."

Leonel laughed as they followed their guide and the blue line leading to the administrative section of the hospital where a catered luncheon awaited.

4

EVELYN IS SHAKEN

Evelyn stared at the numbers moving too slowly on the light up elevator display and scowled at each person who entered or exited and slowed her journey. Every slow-moving, indecisive or physically impaired person in the hospital had ridden in her elevator. Her frustration rose as they stopped on every floor, each delay jangling her already frayed nerves. She needed to get her plan in motion before she lost her nerve.

A tremor moved up her arm. Evelyn grabbed it with her other hand to still it, rubbing the elbow. The tremors had gotten worse, coming more frequently and with more strength. Sometimes it felt like the room shook with her. She hadn't sought treatment, not wanting to waste time in doctor's offices when she could be beside Jeannie's side. She'd self-diagnosed some kind of nerve disorder. Some of her symptoms could be attributed to a psychosomatic response to all the stress of everything going on with Jeannie.

She was trying a phytotherapy package she bought at the farmer's market last summer from a woman who claimed Evelyn's skin, nerve, and mood issues could probably be traced to hormonal imbalances related to menopause. She didn't like the idea she might need such things at only fifty years old, but she had to admit Dr. Liu's supplements helped. Her weird late-life acne had cleared up immediately, and she felt generally calmer. But whenever she got upset, the trembling returned.

And she was upset.

That was all about to improve though. Once she forced the doctors to admit Jeannie into the program, Jeannie would be saved and they could go back to their life together. They'd have to leave Springfield, of course, but they had money enough to set up somewhere else. Maybe they could go to California or Vermont or Canada, or even New Zealand. Anywhere could be home, as long she had Jeannie.

A couple of young people in lab coats got on the elevator next. They didn't glance at Evelyn wedged into a back corner. They chatted happily about being invited to the luncheon with Flygirl and Fuerte.

"He's so handsome," the woman gushed, which made her appear younger than her twenty-five or so years. Her eyes almost disappeared into her round cheeks when she smiled.

"I know," the young man agreed, smiling broadly and revealing teeth badly in need of orthodontic attention. "Do you think they'll demonstrate their abilities? I'd love to see with my own eyes."

The young woman elbowed him in the ribs. "You mean you'd like to see his rippling muscles."

He shrugged. "And? Who wouldn't?"

The two were still laughing when they got off at the third floor. Evelyn could hear them after the doors closed, leaving her blissfully alone. She slumped against the cool metal wall and focused her thoughts, walking through her plan again.

The governor's wife would be in a private room, of course, but they'd need to keep her in the oncology wing. It only made sense they'd house the program with the specialists and trained nursing staff. No one would be suspicious of Evelyn's presence there. She'd practically lived there since Jeannie had been admitted. She needed to explore and figure out where Mrs. Cafry was among all the rooms and labs on the fourth floor.

The next step would be trickier: getting inside her room. She had a few ideas, but the nearer she got to her goal, the more ridiculous they seemed.

She could show her badge from the capitol offices, but she was no longer sure that would get her past the guard or whatever sort of gatekeeper she might encounter.

She hoped to avoid using the gun in her purse. Too much could go wrong with guns. Though she'd taken the safety class and practiced at the range for a month or so, she'd never fired it at anything living. The idea of using it against a human being turned her stomach. Jeannie wouldn't like her using violence either. She was more the "heal the world through love" sort, not a cynic like Evelyn.

And there was the matter of her tremors. The gun could go off accidentally if another round of the shakes overtook her at the wrong moment.

When the doors opened on the fourth floor, she didn't have any clearer idea of how to get into the First Lady's room, and dread ate a hole in her gut.

The hall was emptier than usual. Generally, the place buzzed with activity—nurses and other staff pushing carts up and down the halls and wheeling patients to different areas of the hospital for treatment. But today, only two people lingered in the hall besides herself: a young man crouched on the floor to talk quietly into his phone and a nurse further down the hall, her back to Evelyn.

She guessed she could thank the UCU again. Much of the staff must be at the luncheon with the heroes, making it easier to explore unobserved.

First things first. She went to check in on Jeannie.

Standing outside the door, Evelyn took a moment for a deep breath, then another when the first one came out shaky. She pushed her shoulders down, fluffed her gold-tipped curls, forced a smile onto her face, and opened the door.

She needn't have bothered. Jeannie wasn't awake.

Jeannie lay in her hospital bed, looking impossibly small. Of the two of them, she had always been the larger than life sort. A self-described "big girl," Jeannie had a personality as broad as her hips. Evelyn was much quieter, nicknamed all her life with words like "mouse" and "librarian" and teased for liking imaginary people in books better than real ones.

Finding Jeannie had changed her life, bringing her into a wider, louder world she didn't quite inhabit, but loved all the same. Watching Jeannie at a party was like watching a beautiful tropical bird flying across the room, finding a new perch every few minutes. Gorgeous and kind, everyone loved her. And watching her lying there, quiet and still, ate at Evelyn's heart like acid through steel. She fought back a sob, in case Jeannie simply had her eyes closed. *With all the evil in the world, why would cancer reach out for the good?*

Setting her bag in the visitor's chair, Evelyn walked over to take Jeannie's hand.

Jeannie didn't react, though Evelyn thought maybe her fingers returned the grasp, a pulse more than a squeeze. "I'm going to make them help you." There was fierceness in the whisper. If Jeannie were herself, she'd try to talk Evelyn out of it.

"There's a reason for everything," she'd say. Or, "At least we had each other." Jeannie had been saying too many things lately that sounded like acceptance, like quitting, like letting the doctors give up. But Evelyn refused to believe this was a lost cause. She wanted her miracle. What was the point of living a good life if, in the end, your happiness was snatched out from under you? If being good had gotten her this, then it was time to do something bold, even if it was wrong.

The door to the room bumped open, and a nurse entered. "Oh, hello, Evelyn. Did you remember to sign in?"

Turning to pick up her bag, Evelyn wiped her eyes discreetly and shook her head. "I'll go do that now."

The nurse grabbed her arm as she scooted by, settling her messenger bag and its dangerous contents against her hip. "Did you think any more about hospice? She'd be more comfortable at home."

Evelyn sagged. "I'll talk to the admin this afternoon," she promised, with no intention of doing so.

———

B ack out in the hall, Evelyn signed her name on the clipboard at the desk and wrote Jeannie's name beside it, her handwriting more ragged than usual. Her hand shook, maybe another tremor or maybe fear. She wondered how many times she had signed this roster and how many more times she would before this ended. This might be the last one. Successful or not, she doubted she'd walk onto this floor as a visitor ever again.

A giant bouquet sat on the counter top, daffodils and tulips. Evelyn took a moment to admire it, thinking how to move forward with her plan. She picked up the tag, half-disinterestedly, then realized with a jolt that it was addressed to the governor's wife. "Cafry, room 427." She looked up and down the hall, spotting the number markers with arrows. Before she could talk herself out of it, she marched down the hall, following the arrows to the 400s.

5

JESSICA AND LEONEL DO LUNCH

J essica and Leonel entered the room to the applause of the gathered staff and donors. They turned and looked at each other and Leonel crossed his eyes at Jessica, then they both put on their game faces and walked around shaking hands, signing autographs, and posing for pictures. Suzie had planned the event beautifully. The Director had been wise to hire her. All the same, Jessica wished it was over.

She understood the value in a good public image, especially given some of their other work resulted in things like fires on the college campus and broken masonry in the public square in the center of town. People needed to believe the members of the UCU fought on the side of good and right. She was good at this kind of work, even if it sometimes made her feel cheesy or insincere. She'd be glad when today's glad-handing ended and she could hit the gym to work on pushing her physical limits instead.

Leonel kept rolling his shoulders and trying to pop his neck when he thought no one watched him. He liked a problem he could punch more than diplomacy, but this restlessness seemed unusual. When they were alone, she'd ask about David again.

After the last photos were taken, they all sat down to eat, and, as conversation filled the space with a pleasant buzz of voices, they began to relax a bit. Their table stood apart from the rest, giving them a sense of privacy in the crowded room. Leonel set to work on his chicken right away, amazing Jessica again with his metabolism. Leonel seemed to be always hungry, but never seemed to gain weight or get sluggish from the quantities of food he ate.

It had been a while since they had gotten their families together, and Jessica decided she should invite the Alvarezes over for a movie night or something soon. Things had been tense the last few months between Leonel and his husband.

David didn't like the danger Leonel's work put him in. Especially not after he got shot on the rescue mission to Indiana. But they worked it through, though David was more reserved than previously. He still didn't approve of Leonel's work, but tried to accept it. Otherwise, he'd have to give up on their marriage.

She understood David's worry and Leonel's need for the work. She hoped she and Walter would be able to weather those kinds of storms with half the grace when they arose.

Jessica leaned over to Leonel. "How would you like to be a matron of honor?"

"Does this mean he's asked you?" Leonel set his fork down with a clatter and turned his chair toward her, his face alive with interest.

Jessica grinned, feeling heat rise to her face, but not minding. "I asked him. Walter's shy."

"When?"

"Last night. I haven't told anyone else yet. Except the boys, and my mom, of course. She claimed she already knew. She probably did. She knows everything."

Leonel wrapped an arm around Jessica's shoulders and squeezed gently. "I'm so happy for you both. And, yes! I'll be pleased to be your *dama de honor*. What do your boys say?"

"Frankie gave his approval, along with a warning to Walter that he'd better not hurt me. Max required a bit of explanation about divorce and remarriage and whether this meant that his Daddy wasn't his Daddy anymore, but he likes Walter. I think he'll be excited about it once he works it all out in his mind."

The double doors leading into the room burst open and the room went silent as a young Indian man hurried to the hospital administrator. The administrator listened, then stood, dropping a napkin over his unfinished meal and left quickly, following the man.

"What do you think is going on?" Leonel asked.

"I don't know. But it must be some kind of trouble. I'm sure the bigwigs don't miss something like this for minor considerations."

Leonel stood, walked over to the table where the administrator had been sitting, and offered help. When it was refused, he came back and graciously accepted a large slice of cheesecake from a server who offered one from a tray. Jessica waved hers off. "They said there's some kind of security situation, but their team has it handled."

Jessica sipped her iced tea and gazed out the high windows at the expanse of blue sky open above the fluttering tree branches. She ached to throw herself into the air and zoom among the clouds for a while. Maybe she could get in a little flying this afternoon, after they got back to headquarters. She needed a chance to try out the new uniform and see if the glider wings they'd added helped with directionality at high speeds or if they'd prove an impediment. If she agreed to wear monitors, she might get permission to run a field test over the lake.

In the meantime, though, there was still this banquet to finish. Jessica downed her iced tea and walked over to the doorway where their guide stood. The woman smiled as Jessica approached and leaned in to ask for directions to a bathroom.

T he bathroom was empty when she came in and Jessica took a moment to stretch and bend. She wasn't used to spending so much time in chairs, or with her feet on the ground. Strangely, it seemed to leave her feeling stiffer and wearier than after a mission. Then again, she never had been very good at stillness.

She stretched her arms high over her head and did a sort of half backbend against the wall, then bent down to hug the back of her calves. She hadn't been in this good of shape in years, and she reveled in it. After all she'd put her body through in the past few years—the cancer, menopause, the burns—she'd never imagined feeling this good in her own skin again.

She rolled back a sleeve to trace the gentle scarring left from her skin grafts on what she affectionately termed her "Frankenarm." The body really was an amazing thing, what it could come back from. No one proved that better.

Jessica slipped into one of the stalls to make use of the facilities, careful to protect her "show clothes" in the process. As she slipped her pants back into place, the building shook. *An earthquake?* They were unusual in this part of the world, but not unheard of. She hurried to the sink and washed up, then went back to the meeting hall to see if Leonel had felt it, too.

6

EVELYN IS THE WOLF AT THE DOOR

E velyn found room 427 with little trouble. She'd half expected to hit a second set of security doors or something, but the room was just around the corner with all the others rooms in the 400s. Glancing down the hall, small, bright green cards labeled all the rooms in this section, affixed below the room number. There were no words on the card or numbers. It was subtle, but there had been no green cards next to the room numbers in the 300s or 200s. This had to be the place.

No turning back now. She reached out to try the doorknob, readying an apology and an "I guess I got lost" story in case anyone questioned her presence.

She didn't need it.

The doorknob refused to turn.

She tried again, just in case, but it had the unmistakable stiffness of a locked door. Evelyn looked up and down the hall again, but saw no guards or staff.

A wave of frustration overtook her, and with it, another tremor up her right arm. She rested it against the wall, flattening her palm on the cool tile to still the shaking. The tremor increased until it felt like her whole body shook and the building along with her. Worse than any of the earlier fits, the vibrations made her worry she'd developed a form of epilepsy or suffered some kind of stroke. Her teeth seemed to rattle in her head. Then, as quickly as it began, it ended.

Strangely drained, Evelyn let her body slide down until she sat on the ground, her bag pushed into her ribs and her back resting against the wall. She let her head fall into her hands. Sweat dripped from her brow as if she'd run up all four flights of stairs to get here. She hoped this didn't mean she'd start getting hot flashes as well. She rested a few minutes, thinking.

Obviously staff needed to get through to the special patients, the lucky ones behind this door. So, she had to find out who had a key and get it, one way or another. Pulling herself up to all fours, then standing, she retraced her steps to the front desk where two nurses stood and talked over the counter.

"Evelyn," said the one she'd spoken with earlier. "Did you feel that?"

"What?"

"The earthquake!" said the other nurse, a short, chubby man with a tattoo of Tweety Bird on his forearm.

Evelyn was confused. "I thought it was just me."

"No, there was definitely something. All of us felt it." The chubby nurse pulled a phone from his pocket and clicked something. "I don't think it was an earthquake, though. It seems to have only been here, at the hospital."

"What else could it have been?" The tall nurse put her hands on her hips.

Evelyn chewed her lip, considering. What else, indeed? Her last tremor felt more intense. Was it possible? She pushed the thought away, but it clawed its way back. If Flygirl could fly, what made it so impossible to think she might shake the world? That was one heck of a terrifying idea.

"Evelyn?" The taller nurse laid a hand on her shoulder. "Are you all right? You look like...well, let's say you don't look like yourself, honey."

"I do feel a little shaken up," she admitted.

The nurse slipped an arm around Evelyn's waist and bent her knees so she could offer support under her elbow as well. "Let's find you someplace to sit down for a minute." She called back over her shoulder. "Can you find us some juice? Maybe her blood sugar is low."

Tweety Bird called after them. "Sure thing."

Evelyn felt embarrassed she couldn't remember this woman's name. She recognized her face, and knew her to be kind and sympathetic. Jeannie called her "one of the angels." Luckily, when the woman lowered her into a chair down the hall a bit, Evelyn caught a glimpse of her nametag: Angela. No wonder Jeannie had made the "angel" comment. "Thank you, Angela. I don't know what's wrong with me."

"You don't need to apologize, honey. You have plenty of reason to be shaken up, even before that earthquake or whatever."

Tweety Bird appeared with a cup of juice. "Feeling better?"

Evelyn took the juice and drank it gratefully. It actually did help with the woozy feeling she'd been fighting. "Yes, thank you. That helps."

Tweety Bird leaned over to Angela. "They're ready for you in the green rooms."

Evelyn perked up.

Angela had a key.

Sure enough, Angela stood up and pulled a ring out of her pocket, twisting the keys around until she found one with a green plastic cover over the head. "This won't take long, Evelyn. You sit here as long as you need to and call out if you need help." Then she walked off down the hall, disappearing around the corner to the 400s.

Evelyn watched, then turned back to Tweety Bird. "You must have things to do. I'm fine, really. I'll finish the juice and find my way out. Don't you worry about me."

Tweety Bird examined her face for a moment, and Evelyn concentrated to loosen the tightness of her jaw and appear relaxed. He shrugged. "Well, if you're sure."

"I am."

And with that, he disappeared behind the desk, leaving Evelyn to consider Angela and her keys.

7

JESSICA AND LEONEL SHAKE A LEG

J essica sprang back into the banquet room to find everyone milling about and looking suspiciously at the walls. "I guess it wasn't just me, then?" she said, arriving beside Leonel in the center of the room.

"They don't seem to know what it was."

"Not an earthquake?"

"Not unless you can have an earthquake in only one building." Leonel raised an eyebrow.

"It only happened in this building?" An adrenaline rush flooded Jessica's system. She might do more than shake hands and pose for photos after all.

Leonel nodded, then leaned closer to Jessica. "Do you think this had anything to do with the security situation they didn't want to tell us about?"

Jessica looked around. The administrator and Indian man who had come to fetch him had not returned. But the publicity lady leaned against the wall near the windows. "Let's find out." Giving Leonel a "wait here" gesture, Jessica leaped across the room, realizing too late that the move drew all eyes to her. "Hey. It's Charity, right? Fuerte and

I are due back at headquarters soon. Unless you know of any reason we should stay?"

The woman looked around, wide-eyed.

Jessica pushed her advantage. "The UCU might be able to help. It's not normal, for an earthquake to affect only one building."

"I'm not supposed—"

"You don't have to tell me a thing if it will get you in trouble. But Fuerte—" she waved for Leonel to join them and when he had, continued, "Fuerte has an interest in security systems and would love to have the chance to talk with your team before we leave."

"It's true. Structural integrity is one of my areas of expertise."

Jessica stifled a laugh. Leonel had started his training with the Department by knocking a punching bag through the gymnasium wall, and there had been plenty of jokes about breaking down boundaries and overcoming the walls between people ever since.

Charity's tight expression softened and she rubbed a hand across the back of her neck. "I'm sure I could arrange a tour. Let me call ahead." She scurried across the room, picked up a wall phone and punched in the numbers.

When she came back, she glanced over her shoulder as if expecting to be caught. "No one answered, but I left a message letting them know we're going to drop by. The chief administrator did say to give you the VIP treatment, after all!" The false bright note in her voice jangled in Jessica's ear, but she sympathized with the young woman's position. She and Fuerte would let her follow the letter of her directions and give her deniability about anything that came afterwards.

Leonel stepped into the center of the room and raised his arms high. It only took a moment until the agitated babble dropped to a discontented murmur. "Thank you for the meal and your fine company. It was earth-shaking!"

Polite applause followed the nervous titters as the two made their exit, following Charity. Once through the door, Charity hurried through the halls, seeming to want to get them to the security office before anyone could give her any other directions. Jessica and Leonel followed without a word. Groups of people gathered in each area of the hospital they passed, pointing at the walls.

Luckily, the equipment that kept the hospital functioning seemed unaffected, but each group of hospital employees they passed huddled together. Jessica overheard snatches of frightened theories, "attack" and "terrorist" the most alarming words to jump out at her. Some faces lit up with hope as they made their way through the halls, others darkened with suspicion. How many of the hospital employees blamed Flygirl and Fuerte for bringing some sort of freaky trouble with them?

Jessica didn't know what was going on yet, whether they were about to walk into a weapons situation or some repairman trying to fix an essential building system. She wished she were dressed for work instead of show. When they got back to headquarters, she would insist that even show costumes include protective features and communications gear.

They arrived at security a few minutes later. Charity flung open the door with a flourish and said, "And this is where security keeps track of the happenings of our fine hospital!"

The opening door silenced a conversation among three people standing around a monitor. The picture on the screen showed an African-American woman standing with her hand against a wall. Bent in pain, the woman wobbled as if she might fall, then her body began to vibrate fast enough that the camera image blurred.

For a beat or two, the parties stared at each other, then Leonel stepped forward. "Is this the origin of the earthquake?"

The three security workers all began speaking at the same time, interrupting and shouting over each other, obviously picking up the argument Leonel and Jessica had brought a halt to when they arrived.

"—Just a regular woman—"

"On the watch list—"

"Impossible—"

"Freak—"

"Shaking—"

"Doesn't make sense—"

"Footage doesn't lie—"

Finally, one of the security guards tapped a couple of buttons on the control panel. The image rewound and they watched a middle-aged black woman walk down the hall slowly, hugging her messenger bag against her body and looking at the room numbers. She arrived at the door numbered 427, tried the knob and then seemed to have some kind of fit. One of her arms started shaking. The woman raised it to the wall, pressing her palm flat.

The entire hall started shaking. Light fixtures blinked, paintings tumbled to the floor, and a crack appeared in the wall beside the woman's hand. Her face hidden by a cloud of curls, the woman's body language told a story of fear and pain as she steadied herself.

Afterwards, she slid down the wall, overcome or exhausted.

"Her name is Evelyn Mueller." The youngest of the three guards spoke, a lanky black man who looked like he might have a high school basketball game tonight. An older woman tried to hush him, murmuring something about how the administration would want this kept quiet. He shot her a look and she went silent. "It's Fuerte. Relax. This is what the UCU is for. He'll help."

"I will," said Leonel, stepping forward. "Go on."

"Ms. Mueller is on our watch list. She's family to one of our patients. Had a bit of a violent episode a few days ago, and made some threats. We should have known she was in the building already, but the lobby officers might have been, um, distracted today."

All three guards looked ashamed and Jessica felt embarrassed that her and Leonel's presence provided the distraction.

"Has she exhibited anything like this before?"

"No. She was an ordinary angry woman when we escorted her out. Yelling and lashing out. Nothing like this."

"What floor is that?" Jessica asked.

"Fourth. Oncology."

"Anything special about that area?"

The three security guards exchanged glances. No one spoke.

Charity stepped forward. "Mrs. Cafry's room is back there." They both stared at her blankly, so she added, "The governor's wife."

8

EVELYN IS KEYED UP

Evelyn quickly realized that it was hard to find a place to sit in a hospital and remain unseen. Under the bright fluorescent lights, in the smooth vinyl chairs, she might as well have stood in a police lineup. Not even a rubber plant offered shelter from the cameras and the gazes of passersby. How was she going to get that key without being seen?

She rested in the waiting area where Angela and the Tweety Bird nurse had seated her, sipping her orange juice and thinking. There had to be a way.

On television, when someone needed to sneak around a hospital, they slipped into a closet, found some scrubs or a lab coat, and put them on. When someone stopped the sneaky character, she had to pretend to be a nurse, doctor, or whatever other role the clothes implied.

Evelyn didn't see it playing for comedy here.

Staff reappeared and she guessed the luncheon with the heroes was over. Too bad. They had created a helpful distraction.

Lots of the staff recognized and greeted her as they walked past. That made her presence easy to explain, but didn't make it easy to get away with anything. History wasn't serving her well today. They all knew about the tantrum she'd thrown. They'd probably been asked to keep a special eye on her. She felt a little like that kid at school who always got caught because even the teachers who didn't teach him were watching.

When she no longer felt like her knees would buckle, Evelyn went back to Jeannie's room and watched her chest rise and fall in her sleep for a while. Normally, Jeannie was a light sleeper and Evelyn had to be careful not to roll over too often, but Jeannie hadn't stirred when she entered the room, or when she scooted the table next to the guest chair closer and made a horrible scraping sound.

It was better than the times she had watched Jeannie twitch and moan in her sleep, she supposed, but also worse. Evelyn feared they would never talk again in any real way, that she'd already heard her last "I love you" from Jeannie's lips and hadn't appreciated it.

Evelyn wandered the hall for a little while after that, pretending to examine the art on the walls or to stretch sore limbs, when really she tried to keep track of Angela and her keys. She figured Angela's shift would end soon and she couldn't let her go home without getting those keys.

Watching staff movements for a while, she noticed a room behind the main nurse's desk. From time to time, someone disappeared back there and came back out with a personal item in her hands. A locker room or staff lounge. If she could get in there, she might have a shot at getting those keys.

Her opportunity came a half or so later, when alarms went off in a patient room down the hall. Trying not to think too hard about what the alarms indicated or where they might be coming from, she dashed behind the desk and into the back room.

It took Evelyn's eyes a moment to adjust to the dim light before she could make out the row of lockers and the messy table littered with papers and food items. The slightly darkened room was a relief after spending all day under the hospital's unrelentingly bright lighting. She moved one of the chairs, one of those lightweight armchairs fought over in the waiting room areas, against the door, knowing it wouldn't block anyone entering the room, but hoping it might make noise and give her a warning at least. Then, she started rummaging.

She could have stolen any number of wallets or a nice wad of cash from all the pockets she thrust her hands into. She was surprised how many packs of cigarettes she found. You'd think medical people wouldn't smoke. She found clickers to open at least ten Hondas and Toyotas and that gave her a start of guilt that these people couldn't afford nicer cars. But she didn't find any helpful green-headed keys.

———

She stopped when she heard voices outside the door. It sounded like three or four men talking, then she heard someone, maybe the Tweety Bird nurse saying her name. "Evelyn was just here. Did you look in Waiting Area B? I left her there with some juice a while ago. She'd gotten light-headed. Is anything wrong?"

She couldn't make out what the other voice said, only some masculine mumbling.

This wasn't good. She supposed it could be someone looking for her to talk about hospice arrangements again. But somehow she didn't think so. With all the cameras in the halls, she wondered if her little shaky moment in the four-hundreds wing had been captured and, if it had, what they made of it. She still didn't know what she made of it herself.

Evelyn looked down at her currently steady hands, then wiped them against her jeans as if they were dirty. There had to be some place she could hide in here. None of the lockers could hold a person, even a relatively small one like her. Despite its chairs and the table, there wasn't any place where she could remain hidden for more than a few minutes if someone entered.

There was a door off to her left. She darted through it and found herself in a bathroom. Closing the door, Evelyn locked it and leaned against it for a moment, panic rising in her chest as someone moved around the break room.

Another door connected on the other side of the bathroom. She threw it open and rushed into the adjoining room, a small lab, her triumph mixed with fear as knuckles rapped against the door she'd locked behind her.

Machines lined one wall next to a large, old-fashioned looking desktop computer. A shelf held empty specimen bottles and vials. Luckily for her, the room was empty. Without pausing to explore further, she headed for what looked like another doorway on the other side. Ducking her head through, she quickly ascertained that it was a closet. A dead end.

Her gaze bounced around. There was no place to hide. She was going to get arrested. She'd never get Jeannie the help she needed. Her body began to shake. Not again.

She squatted on the floor, hugging her arms to her body, hoping to ride out the seizure unnoticed.

Luck wasn't on her side.

Someone came into the room.

A few feet away, a pair of white sneaker-clad feet stopped, facing her.

Evelyn looked up.

Angela's face seemed to bob and weave, but she knew her trembling distorted her vision.

"Please," Evelyn said. "You've got to help me."

Angela hurried to squat beside her. "Can you get up?"

Evelyn grabbed Angela's arm and the tremor radiated down through her fingertips and into the other woman's body.

Angela's mouth opened in shock and she shook convulsively. The whole thing lasted only seconds, but for Evelyn, it seemed to take hours.

She was unable to let go of Angela's hand, like the force running through her bound them together. She remembered when her sister had grabbed an electric fence at their grandmother's farm and had stayed there, stuck, unable to let go for long painful seconds, while the current ran through her. Evelyn had tried to tug her sister loose, but ended up shaking with the current, too, until their grandfather had managed to get the girls loose.

This felt the same.

Try as she might, Evelyn couldn't let go. Power pulsed between them, as they shook in time with one another.

Then, it was over.

The shaking stopped.

Angela's face went slack and Evelyn caught her as she fell back, carefully lowering her head to the floor.

Without giving herself time to think about what had happened, or to wonder if she had killed a woman, Evelyn shoved her hand into Angela's pocket and pulled out the keys. Turning them over in her now-steady hands, she found the one with the green head and hurried out the door Angela had entered on the far side of the lab. She had to get back to room 427 before they stopped her.

9

JESSICA AND LEONEL ON THE SCENE

Hovering near the ceiling, Jessica watched the woman on the floor and the other staff gathered around her. The injured nurse, a thirty-something white brunette with long hair pulled into a practical bun, sprawled with her legs spread wide. The crotch of her pink scrub pants was wet where her bladder had let go, but her chest rose and fell, and Jessica saw no sign of blood or physical injury.

Another nurse, a young man with a Tweety Bird tattoo, crouched by her side and helped her sit up. Leonel and the two security guards from the observation room stayed back in the doorway, waiting for her report.

Jessica scooted back to them and lowered herself to the floor, burping discreetly into her elbow to hurry her descent. She wanted to leave the medical professionals space to work. "She's not hurt, at least not visibly."

Leonel pointed to the disarray of specimen jars and other equipment in the room. "Do you think there was a fight?"

Jessica considered. The woman didn't have any bruises or broken skin and she had been alone on the floor with no apparent weapon nearby. The room was a mess, but it didn't look like it had been searched or tossed about by people attacking each other. "No. Nothing is broken or moved far from where it belongs. I think it was another seismic thing."

The woman groaned a little and Jessica floated closer to hear anything she might say. The security guards helped set up a gurney and lift the woman on it. As they settled her in place, the woman whimpered. "Evelyn."

Jessica dropped down by the injured nurse's head, startling the nurse adjusting the rails. She shot him an apologetic look, but leaned over the woman to read her name tag. "Angela? Can you tell us what happened?"

Angela rolled her head toward Jessica and blinked several times. Her eyes went wide and she grabbed the elbow of the nurse with the Tweety Bird tattoo as she rolled up onto her side. He seemed to understand what she meant and thrust a dusty pink kidney-shaped bowl under her face as she threw up. Most of the mucousy yellow spittle landed in the bowl. The nurse took it away and set it on a counter as the woman lay down on her back.

Jessica was not deterred. "Please, ma'am. Anything you can tell us might help."

"I'm not sure." Angela licked her lips several times and shifted her gaze around the room. "Evelyn. She was in here, on the floor. I...I tried to help her, and then, I woke up." A tear carved a line through her makeup. "My head hurts."

The other nurse squeezed the woman's forearm reassuringly. "We'll get you something as soon as we've checked you out."

"Did Evelyn say anything to you?" Knowing their suspect had been here was good information, but knowing what she wanted would be even better.

"She asked me to help her."

"Help her do what?"

"She was shaking." The woman frowned. "I grabbed her arm and then I was shaking, too."

Jessica didn't like the sound of that.

The other nurse jerked his head to indicate Jessica should move out of the way.

She obliged, falling behind the group and into step with Leonel as they followed the gurney into the hall.

"What are you thinking?" Leonel asked.

"It sounds like something freaky to me."

"Me too. Should we call in?"

"Definitely."

When Suzie took their call a few minutes later, she was as quick and to the point as ever. Taking the information they'd gathered about Evelyn Mueller, she immediately set the research team to work, put a team on standby in case things escalated beyond what Flygirl and Fuerte could handle alone, and arranged for heavy duty transport to remove Evelyn from the scene after her capture.

Before the end of the call, Suzie told them Evelyn was married to Jeannie Barbee, a patient at the hospital and about Jeannie's terminal diagnosis. It horrified Jessica that Suzie could get the information so easily, even while she acknowledged the usefulness. Privacy really was an illusion at best.

The nurse with the Tweety Bird tattoo had gone when they came out, his shift apparently over. The new nurse behind the desk, a willowy blonde woman with a permanent scowl, could barely conceal her contempt when approached by the costumed heroes, especially when they signed the visitors log as "Flygirl" and "Fuerte." Still, she directed them to Jeannie Barbee's room.

Ms. Barbee was unresponsive, as the nurse had warned she would be. Standing at the foot of the bed and watching her breathe, Jessica was filled with sympathy for Evelyn and Jeannie. She turned to Leonel. "Put yourself in her shoes. What would you be doing?"

"Anything I could. I'd spend all our money, punch holes in all the walls, and kidnap the President if I thought it would help."

Jessica walked over to the window and looked out at the sunlight

43

sparkling across the cars in the parking lot while she thought. Evelyn Mueller, in the video, had been outside the door of the governor's wife's room. Had that been her plan? To take the woman hostage and use her to leverage a miracle for her own wife?

Jessica spun on her heel and hurried to the hallway in two short bounds. Without looking to see if Leonel followed, she flew the short distance and dropped down in front of the front desk again, startling the grumpy blonde. "Who has keys to Mrs. Cafry's room?"

The woman stared at her, carefully blank-faced. Jessica groaned in frustration. She wasn't going to tell them anything.

A door closed behind them, and the young security guard from downstairs stood in the hall, sliding his hat back onto his head. Jessica leaped to his side in a single bound, and he grinned, thrilled by Jessica's abilities. "Who has keys to Mrs. Cafry's room?" she asked.

He looked around. The other security guard was nowhere to be seen, probably searching for Evelyn Mueller. He leaned down to whisper. "Security, of course. Other than that, only the medical staff who need access to the clinical research rooms."

"Like Nurse Angela?"

He looked at the door he'd just come through, a troubled expression crossing his face. "Yes."

"Find out if she still has her keys."

EVELYN MAKES THE EARTH MOVE UNDER HER FEET

E velyn wished she had thought to take one of the scrub shirts or jackets from the break room. The TV ploy that seemed ridiculous a half hour ago didn't seem so silly now. It might, at least, have made her a little more invisible. Instead she cowered in corner after corner, paranoia ratcheted up, afraid of what might happen if anyone tried to stop her.

God, she hoped Angela was okay. The nurse had been nothing but kind to her over the months of Jeannie's treatments, and Evelyn had no desire to hurt her. She hadn't known what would happen.

If she understood her own situation, she would seize control of it. But, the tremor in her arm indicated more than a neurological problem. Generally, a person with a tremor suffered embarrassment and had trouble holding onto things. They didn't shake walls and put other people into convulsive fits.

Please, she prayed to God, who had ignored all her prayers so far. *Please let her be all right.*

Despite the gun in her bag, Evelyn didn't want to hurt anyone. All she wanted was a chance for her Jeannie, even a slim one.

Slipping into an alcove that housed several of the carts nurses used to check vitals, she pressed herself against the wall and tried to get her bearings. Having come through the rat's maze of labs and back rooms of the oncology ward, she wasn't sure where on the floor she had come out. She pulled her messenger bag around and dug out some tissues to mop her face and blow her nose. In doing so, her hand brushed the gun. She recoiled as if bitten by a snake.

She wasn't any less desperate to save her wife, but what she might have to do in order to get Jeannie the help she needed terrified her. Hurting Angela might only be the beginning of the violence she would commit. But she would go to hell if that was what it took to keep Jeannie alive.

What was her love worth if she wasn't willing to go all the way? Jeannie had always said she loved Evelyn because she meant what she said. She still meant it, no matter how much it scared her.

Footsteps in the hall and the crackle of radio chatter.

Evelyn held her breath, waiting for the moment someone called out or a hand grasped her arm to pull her out of her hiding place, but the steps passed and echoed as the security guard or whoever kept walking.

Evelyn scooted to the edge of her hiding place, turning her head slowly until one eye peeked around the corner at the hall.

When she didn't see anyone, she dared to lean out, trying to read the wall signage. Her vision seemed cloudy, like she had something in her eyes. She blinked hard, trying to bring the plaques into focus. Finally, she made out a number: 311.

So, she'd come out in the 300s. Good. Far away from the front desk, at least. Now, which way to the 400s from here?

Evelyn wiggled her fingers into her jeans pocket and found the keys from Nurse Angela's pocket still wedged there. She couldn't see anything to clue her in as to whether she should turn right or left, so she stepped into the hall and turned right, away from the person with the radio.

It didn't take long for her to realize she was going the wrong way. The next room number was smaller instead of larger.

Shit.

There was nothing to be done. She turned around and almost walked straight into a large man's chest.

The man wore a red shirt, flashy for a hospital visit, but not the dark blue security staff uniform.

She tilted her head up and looked into the face of a man wearing a mask resembling half of a golden sun.

Fuerte.

She recognized him immediately, of course. Even spending all her time at the hospital, she'd seen his image on the news and talk shows. If he chose, this man could pick her up and break her in half. But he didn't seem to want to hurt her. Instead, he held his hands up to his sides and looked at her with velvety brown eyes, soft and kind. "Evelyn?" he said, voice as soft as those eyes.

Her throat seemed to pinch off like the end of a balloon, leaving her only able to squeak. "You've got to let me through."

"I can't do that." He sounded genuinely sad like he wanted to help her, but couldn't.

When he reached toward her, she backed away. "Don't touch me!" She held her right arm between them, and they both saw when it began to quake.

"Evelyn, please, let me help you. I know you don't want to hurt anyone."

She glared at the man. "Who are you to tell me what I want?"

Fuerte looked over his shoulder at the empty hall behind him, then turned his gaze back to her. "Jeannie wouldn't want this."

Evelyn was shocked he would talk about Jeannie, and her shock turned to rage. Just like a man, to assume he knew best, to try and tell her what to do. She lurched toward him, her arm quavering in the air in front of her.

He evaded her, but managed to block her path. She lunged and when he dodged, she ended up sprawled on the floor. The contents of bag spilled, including the gun.

She grabbed it with her left hand, shoving it back into her bag as she pulled herself to her knees, careful to keep from touching the walls or the floor with her still-trembling right hand. The shaking intensified, her own hand a blur, moving too fast to follow.

Fuerte spread his hands in what was probably supposed to be a conciliatory gesture, but only accentuated the breadth of his chest and the size of his muscles. "Violence isn't going to solve anything," he said. His body built for violence, he presumed to tell her to take the way of peace?

"Maybe not," she said. "But it will definitely make me feel better." She leaned forward, touched her hand to the floor and willed the motion forward and away from her. The floor shook and began to buckle, forcing Fuerte to struggle to keep his feet. She wiggled her palm from side to side and the entire hall shook. Fuerte bounced against the wall. "Get out of my way." The words came between gritted teeth and the floor buckled around Fuerte's feet, dropping him into a hole that appeared in the floor.

He hung there, suspended, holding his torso out of the opening with those arms. "Evelyn, don't do this!"

She sat one moment longer, then scrambled to her feet and ran down the hall without looking back, half-blinded by her own tears.

JESSICA AND LEONEL SPLIT UP

When Jessica arrived a few moments later, Leonel had pulled himself out of the hole in the floor. Plaster dust covered his pants and shirt and he tried to wipe it off with hands also covered in dust. Jagged sections of floor poked up at odd angles, a mess of wires jutted out and occasional sparks flew into the air.

Jessica floated over the hole and ducked her head inside. Besides the chunk of the ceiling on the floor below, it didn't look like anyone had been hurt, at least not that she could see. Jessica rolled into a loop-the-loop and landed softly on the intact section of floor near her friend.

"She went that way," he said, pointing down the hall.

Jessica stood and coiled against the wall, planning to use it to shove off and give her a faster start.

"Wait! She has a gun."

Jessica let her leg slide back down to the floor, crouching with her fingers templed between her knees. Neither of them was bulletproof and their show uniforms weren't equipped with the Kevlar panels built into the real work suits. Jessica had already seen the trauma a bullet wound could inflict when Leonel got shot during the mission in

Indiana. She wasn't interested in experiencing that sensation first-hand. Nor was she interested in letting it happen to someone else. They could use a bulletproof lizard woman on their team right about now. But Patricia didn't do the Good Will missions.

Patricia was your woman in a fight, but preferred to leave politicking and glad-handing to those who weren't fed up with tact and pussyfooting around. "Think of me as a hammer," she liked to say. "Call me when you have some nails that need pounding." The UCU staff only half joked when they said she didn't have the heart.

They'd have to find another way to stop this woman, one that didn't end with Evelyn shooting someone before shaking the hospital to the ground. Her antics had done enough damage in the past few hours.

Leonel pulled himself up at the sound of feet running up the hall toward them from the 200 wing. "Stop!"

The two guards skidded a little as they tried to come to a sudden halt.

Leonel stretched out an arm to assist, taking the impact of the two men against his arm without giving ground. It clotheslined them and knocked them on their bottoms, but they hadn't fallen through the hole in the floor.

"Radio your team," Leonel said. "Evelyn is heading for the 400s wing. She's armed as well as dangerous."

Leonel stretched out on his stomach to look into the hole in the floor at the giant chunk of material taking up most of the hallway of the 300 wing of the third floor. "Please tell me no one was under that."

The floor creaked and moaned beneath his weight and Leonel snaked his body backwards before rolling up onto his knees.

Jessica dove into the hole. Once on the floor below, she squatted next to the chunk of ceiling and looked underneath. The lighting on the third floor had gone dark, but streaming sunlight allowed her to make out that there was nothing to see. She looked up and made a thumbs-up gesture at Leonel. "Clear."

"*Gracias a Dios.*"

Another quick glance around showed that emergency lighting flickered on. Jessica decided to trust to the hospital's emergency systems to deal with the needs of the patients on this floor. Her responsibility was to her team first, and to stop Evelyn before she could do more harm.

When Jessica floated up, Leonel backed up slowly, trying not to cause additional damage to the floor. Jessica didn't land, instead hovering some inches above where the floor should be. The security guards were still having a back and forth over their radios with the rest of the team.

"I'm going after her," Jessica said.

Leonel nodded. "I figured as much. Be careful." He picked up a chunk of the floor and moved it against the wall. "I'm going to help shore this up."

Jessica let her body rise until she was parallel to the ceiling a few inches below the lights and pushed herself as fast as she dared in such a confined space. Evelyn had already had several minutes to get ahead. Communications had been patchy to the 400s wing since the first earthquake, so Jessica didn't know if she had any allies ahead or not. She rounded the corner, automatically bending at the waist to mitigate the pull to the side and avoid losing speed.

The empty hall stretched before her. That wasn't good news. Evelyn must already be through the door with her intended victim. Jessica didn't know what the woman had in mind. Murder, blackmail, hostage-taking, or something else entirely, but she had to get in there and stop her. Door number 427 was solid, with no glass panels to peek through. Jessica landed softly to the right of the door, then flipped herself upside down as she tried the knob. It turned readily, and nothing happened. No gunshot rang out, no trembling shook the building.

Floating back up, Jessica nosed over the top of the door, trying to peek into the space beyond. She couldn't make out much. There appeared to be a short hallway leading to a secondary doorway. Jessica snaked over the top of the door trying not to let herself dip more than a few inches, staying high and out of view. "No one looks up," her trainer always told her.

"Who's there?" a tremulous voice called out.

Jessica froze, spread against the ceiling like a spider.

A woman peered around the doorframe that led to Mrs. Cafry's room. Most of her body remained hidden behind the door, but long fingers gripped the doorframe, and dark curls surrounded a round face screwed up in concentration.

From above, the woman appeared shorter and squatter than the cameras had shown, but Jessica still recognized Evelyn Mueller. She looked more fragile than Jessica expected for a woman who had wreaked so much havoc in her quest to get this far.

"Is it the nurse?" A second voice called out from the room beyond.

Evelyn turned around. "I guess there's no one there."

Jessica held her breath and waited for Evelyn to return to the room.

EVELYN TAKES HER STAND

E velyn closed the door and sat in the visitor's chair again, letting her head fall into her hands. This wasn't how she'd thought it would be at all. She'd expected there to be someone to fight, a guard to overcome. She'd expected Mrs. Cafry to be imperious and intimidating, as always, facing down the press or her husband's detractors.

Instead, she'd broken into the fortress to find a room with eight women resting in hospital beds. She wasn't sure at first which one, if any, might be Mrs. Cafry. No one looked like the right person. No one stood guard over them, not even a nurse. She guessed that made sense. The staff had probably all been called to deal with the damage she'd caused.

A wave of guilt at the thought of other patients endangered by her recklessness made Evelyn want to vomit. Between the nausea and the weakness in her limbs from her escape from Fuerte, she feared she didn't have the strength to see this through, that she'd come this far only to fail.

The patients had all turned their eyes to her when she entered, regarding her passively as various monitors and machines blipped, beeped, and wheezed quietly. One woman's face was red and wet as if she'd been crying. Another barely spared her a glance before letting her head roll back on the pillow to regard the ceiling.

Evelyn slumped in her seat and stared right back at all the bald, slender women in their beds.

Finally one of them spoke.

"Can I help you?"

Evelyn recognized Mrs. Cafry's voice. Her modulated contralto proved the only recognizable thing about her. Her trademark blonde coif, reminiscent of Doris Day updated for the new century, was gone. She wore no makeup and, without it, her skin seemed green, though that might have been the lighting. Evelyn probably looked green under these lights. Jeannie did, green-gray like an army footlocker and nearly as battered.

Then Evelyn began to cry. "I don't think you can. I don't think anyone can."

"Sh-sh-sh-sh." Someone let out a soothing hiss.

Mrs. Cafry studied her calmly, large blue eyes shining with sympathy. "You're not supposed to be here, miss. No one is supposed to be here without a mask."

Evelyn put a hand over her nose and mouth, as if she hadn't come into the room with a gun in her purse and every intention of hurting this woman. Faced with a helpless woman lying in a hospital bed instead of the powersuit-wearing former debutante she'd pictured, Evelyn was horrified at herself. What good would come of threatening her?

Then, she thought of Jeannie.

She pushed her shoulders and her fears down and stepped nearer to Mrs. Cafry's bed. "What are they doing with you in here?"

"It's a cancer study. A drug they haven't tried on me yet. The other treatments aren't doing it."

Evelyn tried to remember what the research team had said about this program, about why Jeannie didn't qualify for the experimental drugs, too. The conversation with the doctor seemed foggy, like she had listened with cotton stuffed in her ears. She couldn't remember details, just the sad look on the woman's face as she shook her head.

She shoved the memory away and crossed her arms over her chest. "So, they think they can save you?"

"We're hoping so."

A long silence fell. Beads of sweat formed on Evelyn's forehead and dripped down her cheeks. She wiped them away with the back of her hand and held her fingers in front of her face. They trembled. She shoved her hand into her jeans pocket and wrapped her other arm around herself. But she could feel the tremor growing. She bit the inside of her cheek and concentrated.

Mrs. Cafry gasped. "What in the world?"

Evelyn followed her gaze to the ceiling in time to spot a booted foot coming toward her head. She dodged, and it grazed the side of her jaw instead of taking her squarely. She grabbed at the bed frame for support, pulling her trembling right hand free from her pocket. When she touched it to the floor to right herself, the entire room lurched and all the women called out in fright and pain. Some of the monitor alarms went off. Evelyn immediately lifted her hand into the air, holding it up as if waving at someone. It jittered for another second or two.

Back on her feet, Evelyn turned in a circle, looking for the person who had attacked her, but didn't see anyone. "I don't want to hurt anyone!" she called out. "But I will, if I have to."

"I don't want anyone to get hurt, either." The calm and quiet voice came from behind.

Evelyn spun, nearly losing her balance.

Flygirl hovered in the middle of the room.

Impossible.

Evelyn felt her eyes grow wide with shock and amazement, but she couldn't help it. Some part of her must have always thought it a trick, a stunt involving camera angles and wires. People could not really fly. Yet Flygirl floated in the center of the room like some kind of red-haired, blue and white clad balloon.

It simply couldn't be.

Of course, people couldn't cause earthquakes with their bodies, either.

At least they shouldn't be able to.

Evelyn looked at her hand again, grateful to find it still for the moment.

Flygirl spoke again. "Let me help you. There are people who understand this kind of thing, who can help you control what's happening to you."

"What's happening to me?" Evelyn blinked. This wasn't about her own problems. This was about Jeannie. "What about what's happening to her?"

Even behind the mask, the confusion in Flygirl's eyes was easy to read. "To her?"

"To my Jeannie. These people, these so-called doctors…they're letting her die. Here in this room, they're trying something else for these women. If they do it for the governor's wife, why can't they try and save my Jeannie-girl, too? Is she not good enough for them?"

"I don't know why Jeannie's not getting this treatment, Evelyn. But I'm sure the doctors are doing everything they can for her."

"What if that's not good enough?"

"Not good enough?"

"You heard me. What if they do everything and that's not good enough? Am I supposed to let them let her die?" Evelyn's hand shook so quickly now, it blurred in the periphery of her vision. She grabbed for Flygirl with it, but the costumed woman darted out of reach, hovering near the ceiling. Evelyn jumped, but she'd never been an athlete and it only extended her reach a couple of inches.

Evelyn thrust her left hand into her messenger bag. She was right-handed, but she'd have to manage somehow. Her right hand couldn't be relied on to obey her commands. After fumbling for a moment, she pulled out the gun. It felt very heavy in her left hand, but she trained it on Flygirl anyway. "They are going to save her, or die trying."

LEONEL MAKES HIS OWN WAY

Another tremor shook the floor, and Leonel reached out to grab the arm of the security guard before he could fall through the hole into the level below them. The lights flickered and the radio on the guard's hip crackled. The jagged break in the floor widened. Leonel knew they had to get Evelyn Mueller out of the hospital before she razed the place. The potential for damage in a building like this one, where delicate equipment kept patients breathing and monitored, had Leonel's heart racing. So far, the generators seemed to be keeping up, but additional structural failure would tax the resources beyond capacity.

Feeling ponderous, heavy, and useless, Leonel stood looking down the hall where Jessica had flown. Any attempt to cross the hole in the middle of the fourth floor would only make the instability worse, dropping additional chunks of the building into the third floor hallway. "Is there another way over there?"

"Not on this floor."

Of course.

Leonel looked into the hole. He thought about jumping in, but he might further damage the third floor and cause slabs of ceiling to rain down on the second like highly destructive dominos. Even leaning into the hall made something creak and moan. He should go back and take the stairs, down and across the third floor, then up on the other end. Too much time around Jessica had him ignoring ordinary ways of life sometimes. "We need to get this stabilized."

As if in answer, the floor groaned. The group backed further down the hallway. One of the guards grabbed Leonel's arm. "We've got to get these people out of here." He pointed at the rooms down the hall, where medical staff, visitors and some patients peered around corners.

Leonel took another look down the hall where Jessica had disappeared, trying to trust that her training would keep her safe as she took on Evelyn Mueller alone. He had to see to the safety of the patients and staff. "What's your evacuation plan?"

"We get everyone transferred to Springfield Memorial."

Leonel laid a hand on the man's shoulder, careful to touch him gently, but still knocking him forward. He helped steady the smaller man. "Radio it in. Let's get started."

Leaving a guard on each side of the gaping hole to make sure no one ventured too close, Leonel set off down the hall back the way he had come. He stopped the first person in scrubs he saw. "This part of the building is unstable. We need to evacuate these people. How difficult is that going to be?"

"In this wing? The patients are mostly ambulatory."

"Good. Get them downstairs and out of the building. I need to make a phone call."

Suzie answered immediately. With a few succinct questions, she grasped the situation. "I'll coordinate transport and emergency services. Leave this part to us, Leonel. You get to Jessica."

When Leonel emerged from the office where he'd made the phone call, the hallway was full of people. Staff directed patients and their families to the stairwells at the end of the hall and organized those who couldn't take the stairs.

"Is there another stairwell?" he asked a passing nurse.

She shook him off annoyed, then froze when she saw who asked. "Fuerte?" She sounded more puzzled than impressed.

"Please, ma'am. It's imperative I get to the other side of this building."

She gaped at him.

"And quickly," he added.

"We're using all the staircases to evacuate. You can't get through right now."

Leonel strode toward the main stairwell. A quick glance over the heads of the people still crowding the hall showed him a stairwell full of carefully moving people. Murmuring excuses, he moved to the middle of the landing and peered down. The staircases spiraled around a center surrounded with metal railings, typical in institutions, giving the staircase as small a footprint as possible. The gap between one flight and the next was rectangular, but definitely wide enough for a man to fit. And Leonel was going to be that man.

He gripped the edge of the metal railing and tugged gently. He prayed the construction had not taken short cuts as he climbed over and lowered himself down. These railings had to support him. He could feel the crowd on the stairwell watching him and heard the excited chatter. So far as any of them knew, Springfield had fallen victim to a series of earthquakes that de-stabilized the building. He wanted to let them keep thinking the only danger they faced was from Mother Nature and not a madwoman taking hostages. Panic helped no one in an evacuation.

Ignoring them, Leonel hung as low as his arms allowed, then looked around. The railing rose higher on the left side, at the top of the flight of stairs, so he monkey-barred around until his feet aligned with it.

The thump of his landing frightened a small Hispanic woman. "Discúlpame, Señora," he said, bowing his head. Crouching on the railing beside her, he brought his hands between his knees to grasp the handrail and lowered his body into the gap again, careful not to squeeze the metal too tightly and break it. Thank goodness for the show costume's flexible material, or he'd have shown everyone his underwear. Finally, he thumped onto the third floor landing harder than he'd intended, startling the evacuees.

It wasn't difficult to work his way through the crowd spilling into the stairwell, at least not once people saw who wanted through. The notoriety that came with the mask served its purposes sometimes. Once clear of the crowd, he ran hard until he got to the middle of the third floor hall. He prayed the roundabout path would get him back to the other side of the building in time to help Jessica.

14

JESSICA TRIES TO HELP

J essica held her hands out placatingly. "You don't want to do this, Evelyn."

"Want?" She laughed. "Since when is any of this about what I want?"

Jessica's heart plummeted. "What about Jeannie?"

"Jeannie?" A tear rolled down Evelyn's cheek. "No. This isn't about what she wanted either. We wanted to grow old together." She swung her arm and the gun in it wildly.

The women in the beds gasped.

Jessica swooped through the air and Evelyn trained the gun back on her. Not ideal, but it would keep the woman from shooting one of the patients by mistake. Despite the training the Department provided, Jessica felt completely unprepared to deal with the situation, but her first duty was to protect the people in the room. She had to trust Leonel was doing what he could for the rest of the hospital.

"Let's talk about what's going on with you." Jessica lowered herself slowly to the floor and stepped toward the armed woman. "These tremors in your arms are more than a muscle control problem, aren't they?"

"What would you know about it?"

"Plenty. You think I could control my movement like this the first time I tripped and didn't fall?"

Evelyn stared at her blankly, but the rigidity in the arm holding the gun relaxed a little.

"I had to be taught. We can teach you, too."

"We?"

"The UCU. You're not the first woman to have unusual problems in our city."

Evelyn swayed a little on her feet. She still had her right hand jammed firmly into her pocket, the elbow spasming at her side. "It's happening again, isn't it?" Jessica reached out, not sure what she could do, but wanting desperately to help.

"No! Don't touch me!"

Jessica pulled her hand back, remembering Nurse Angela. Touching Evelyn Mueller while her body quaked was not a good idea.

Evelyn dropped to the floor and laid the gun between her knees. She pulled her hand free of her pocket and pinned it against her torso with her other arm. Her entire body quaked, and the room seemed to roll with it.

All the women in their beds groaned. One began to whimper.

Jessica crept closer, kneeling to look into Evelyn's pained face. Her mind raced, trying to find a way to get Evelyn somewhere she couldn't cause any more harm.

Another tremor shook the entire floor.

Jessica floated off the ground to avoid being thrown about.

Evelyn groaned. "Help me!" she cried, her voice distorted by the shaking. "I can't make it stop."

LEONEL HOLDS IT TOGETHER

T he center of the third floor was a mess. Thick slabs of concrete lay on the floor where they had broken amid sections of foam ceiling tile. Loose wiring hung through the gaping hole overhead, but nothing sparked or steamed anymore. The entire area was buried in debris and the air seemed thick with pulverized concrete, sheet rock, and tile. Scarier yet was the crack in the floor, suggesting the whole thing might be about to drop through to yet another level of the hospital.

As Leonel arrived on the scene, the building rocked again. Screams echoed in the stairwells at both ends. The lone security guard left to ensure no one passed this direction shot Leonel a desperate look.

"Get out of here," Leonel said.

The young man didn't say anything in return, but turned and scurried down the hall, disappearing from view.

A groaning sound gave the only warning before another large chunk of the fourth floor fell toward Leonel. He bent and caught it on his back and shoulders, then slowly lowered it to the floor, as far from the crack in the middle as he could. The building seemed to wheeze like an asthmatic climbing a hill. Before his eyes, the split in the floor grew. Leonel could imagine the two sides of the structure collapsing, killing everyone still in the stairwells at the two ends. There had to be something he could do.

Leonel only had had two years in the field, but he had already learned that protocol offered nothing more than a leaping off point, that when the crisis came, you had to make a decision and react, hoping for the best. So, that's what he did.

Climbing the nearest pile of debris, he got within reach of the dangling rebar supports now visible. He bent a piece around to form a hook-shaped handle. He hurried to the other side to do the same with the hunks of metal hanging there.

Preparations done, he pushed a large chunk of fallen concrete to the center and, crossing himself and sending a quick prayer to *La Virgen*, he set to work. He tried not to imagine the extra weight straining the damaged floor below. With a slow breath to center his concentration, Leonel climbed atop, reaching and grabbing the two handles he'd made and drawing them near each other like the two sides of a cable fly machine in the UCU gym.

The Department had yet to find the limits of Leonel's physical strength and he hoped this would not be the day he discovered he wasn't strong enough. He had thrown cars and torn steel doors off their hinges. Surely, he could bring together two pieces of rebar and tie them in a knot.

He pulled.

The angle was difficult. He struggled to keep purchase on the ragged chunk of concrete that boosted him to the right height, but Leonel Alvarez didn't give up easily. Jamming a boot against the concrete to steady himself, he refocused and tried again.

Slowly, the two sides of the torn floor drew nearer each other. Leonel's muscles strained like nothing he had done before. He breathed out loudly, automatically using the patterns he had learned in Lamaze childbirth classes so many years before in another life. *Pant-two-three-four-blow. Pant-two-three-four-blow.* He leaned back adding the strength of his back and abdomen to the tremendous pull. His gripping fists drew nearer each other in increments, until, at last, metal clicked against metal.

Leonel wound the pieces of rebar around each other in a version of a sheet bend knot. When his trainer taught him these knots, they'd talked about wilderness survival and emergency rigging, rappelling and subduing invaders. Neither had imagined using the techniques to keep a building from falling down, but he hoped these materials would respond to the forms. It was the best idea he had.

One knot in place, he ran back and forth making more sets of rebar knots, holding the east and the west sides of the building together and praying the stop-gap would keep the building up long enough to get the people out.

16

EVELYN ISN'T TOO LATE

Jeannie always used to say it was never too late. "After all, we found each other. Right, baby?"

Jeannie had been thirty when Evelyn met her at the library book club. Evelyn had been thirty-five. They caught each other's eye when an older white woman tried to express how uncomfortable Celie and Shug made her feel in The Color Purple. "It's almost like they're in love, but that can't be right, can it?"

Oh, yes it could.

And it had been right.

Secretly, Evelyn thought Jeannie's relentless optimism cute, but she'd never bought into it herself. The world was a dark and ugly place most of the time, especially for a black lesbian in a Southern city. Holding onto bitterness proved difficult when you shared your life with a woman who tasted only sweetness. Evelyn had changed in her years with Jeannie, found a kind of optimism within herself, too, but all tied up in her love for the woman dying on the other side of the building. Without her, she had no idea how to find hope.

"It's not too late," Flygirl said. She sounded strange, like she spoke from the other side of a wall, muffled and warbled.

Evelyn tried to look her in the face, but it was like trying to focus on one image in a kaleidoscope. The effort made her nauseated. She shook her head and closed her eyes, but it didn't help. Her own body generated the shaking and she didn't know how to make it stop. She groaned, bending toward the floor, still understanding that she must not let her shaking hand touch. It didn't make any sense, but her seizures, or whatever they were, could shake a room apart and she didn't want to do that. Jeannie wouldn't want her to hurt anyone, not even to save her life. It wasn't too late to give up this crazy plan, to walk away. It couldn't be too late.

"Breathe." The voice came softly in her ear.

She thought for a moment it might be her mother, though that didn't make sense. Her mother had been gone a long time now. Still, she tried to obey. She rocked back and forth, straining to pull in a long, calming breath. The best she seemed to be able to do was to pant.

"Breathe," the voice said again.

Evelyn drew in a raggedy breath, more a gasp than a pant, but it hurt less. She tried again.

"Think about clouds drifting in a pale blue sky. Waves lapping a sandy shoreline. Breathe."

Flygirl's voice, clearer now, had taken on a soothing tone, like one you might use with a child, but Evelyn didn't feel insulted. She could feel her body stilling. The quakes were gentler, like they had been at the beginning. A trembling in the hand and arm, a feeling of vertigo. The room stilled and the women in it panted with her.

"Do you think you can stand?"

Evelyn looked at Flygirl, still hovering in the air. With the light behind her from the window, she glowed like some kind of saint. She wanted to answer her, but instead, she slumped to the floor.

17

WHAT THEY SAW AND DIDN'T SEE

Leonel leaned against a wall, panting, and surveyed his work. The two halves of the fourth floor above him were tied to each other, creaking and moaning, but holding, at least for now. The crack in the third floor had not widened. It wouldn't withstand another serious quake, but there hadn't been any more while he worked. He dared to hope it would keep the building in one piece until they could get everyone out.

Springfield Women's Hospital had always seemed small to Leonel, after the larger hospitals where he'd kept vigil over his mother during her final months. But now, he worried he hadn't bought the firemen and security guards and other workers enough time to get everyone out safely. There seemed to be so many people.

Leonel moved the large chunks of cement he'd used as scaffolding away from the damaged area of the floor, so their weight didn't put additional strain on the damaged structure. Then, he dusted his hands on his pants and sprinted toward the stairwell at the opposite end of the hall.

No one remained in the hall waiting to get into the emergency stairs and Leonel sighed. Maybe the fourth and third floor denizens had all gotten out.

He plunged into the stairwell and flung himself up the stairs as fast he could go, fear rising in his chest. Maybe Jessica had not been able to subdue Evelyn alone. What if he had failed her?

He burst onto the fourth floor and a team of security guards and police officers all trained their guns on him.

He raised his hands. "It's all right. I'm here to help."

The young security guard who had helped from the start emerged from the middle of the crowd. No one tried to stop him. All the officers looked tense; a few looked frightened. "She's in there," the young guard said, pointing at the closed door they'd clustered around. "So are eight patients."

Leonel pulled himself upright, forcing confidence into his voice. "So is Flygirl."

They all stood still, listening, but heard nothing.

Leonel wished desperately for the radio-linked earpieces he and Jessica always wore on missions. If he made it through this, he was going to demand safety and communication features in the show gear. No one had expected them to save lives today, but that didn't change what was happening now. "I'm going in," Leonel announced. "Ms. Mueller is in possession of a firearm. Does anyone have a vest I can use?"

"You need one?"

"I am not bulletproof," Leonel admitted, trying not to relive getting shot in Indiana. That wasn't an experience he cared to recreate.

The crowd of safety workers murmured, then a police officer stepped forward, removing his Kevlar vest. The man was smaller than Leonel, but the largest among them.

Leonel thanked him with a bow of his head and loosened the adjusters to get as much play as possible. He strapped the protective gear into place. It wasn't anywhere near as good as the gear built into his work uniform, but reassuring all the same.

He walked up, standing to the side of the door and waited for another officer to open it. The other man yanked the door open, bouncing it against the wall so hard it nearly slammed shut again. The group let out its collective breath when nothing happened.

SAMANTHA BRYANT

A narrow hall led to the room beyond with limited visibility. Leonel could make out standard hospital tile on the floor, but nothing more. For all he knew, everyone in the room was dead. He crossed himself once again, kissed his fingers and held them to the sky. He burst into the hall, flinging himself in a random pattern: crouching, standing, and rolling from side to side. His trainers would have been proud.

Finally, he rolled into the room and, looking up from his crouch on the floor, found eight women in hospital beds staring at him with wide, frightened eyes. Jessica knelt on the floor beside the prone Evelyn Mueller. He scrambled to her side.

"Get her out of here," Jessica said.

Without stopping to ask questions, Leonel scooped the limp woman into his arms, cradling her against his chest and sped from the room. Sweat soaked Evelyn's shirt and her makeup was a ruin of caked layers. "It will be all right," he told her, not knowing if she could hear him.

The stairwell was blessedly clear. Only a few firemen and other safety officers remained and they moved aside as he ran past, trying to keep his stride even and steady to not jostle Evelyn. He burst into the outdoors and stopped, not knowing where to take her.

The image of him standing with Evelyn Mueller in his arms ran on all the news channels. Reports called Evelyn mentally ill or a terrorist, depending on which network the coverage came from. Most praised Flygirl and Fuerte for their efforts to protect and evacuate the patients and staff. Suzie didn't share the ones blaming the UCU for causing the damage or failing to act quickly enough.

No one had footage of the private ambulance that took Evelyn Mueller away to a specially prepared room at the Department. No one had pictures of the two heroes, masks finally removed, arms around each other for comfort as they rode back to headquarters in an unmarked van. No one saw how fiercely they hugged their families when they got home.

When Flygirl visited Jeannie in the hospital, she went as Jessica Roark, and no one was the wiser.

THE END

.

II

FRIEND OR FOE

1

CINDY LIU, ESCAPE ARTIST

You're going to have to sit down, miss."

Cindy Liu whirled around, a retort ready to fly—who was this man to tell her to sit down? —and found the driver turned around in his seat and scowling at her. Thinking fast, she arranged her face into her best impression of a frightened, young girl. It wouldn't do to get kicked off the bus before she'd made her escape. She thought she could still see Patricia on the sidewalk, despite the emergency vehicles crowding the street. There wasn't nearly enough distance between her and trouble yet.

"Sorry, sir," she said, pitching her voice high and flashing a nervous smile at the man.

She plopped into the seat imitating adolescent acquiescence and primly folded her hands in her lap. The driver nodded and turned back around in his seat when the light turned green. The last beams of sunset still pierced the horizon as the bus took the entrance ramp to the highway. Cindy was on her way.

Not the most auspicious start she'd ever had, but she had reclaimed the emeralds and escaped from Patricia O'Neill and friends. The authorities would have descended on the college campus by now and, if luck was on her side, they would spend hours or even days explaining themselves. After all, the truth was hardly credible. Women who could fly, wield fire, and transform themselves into giant bipedal lizards? A story like that would land them in a hospital talking to the rubber walls. Cindy would be long gone by then, on her way to straightening out the mess her life had become. It had all gone wrong so fast. It didn't even seem possible.

There would be time to worry about how it had gone wrong later. Time to move forward and figure out where she could go from here. She didn't have much with her, just the clothes on her back and the meager contents of her wallet. Money would be her first priority. Maybe Helen could help. No. Helen hadn't made it out. She'd left Helen back there, with them, imprisoned or maybe even dead. Cindy was really on her own, all her best allies left behind. She'd think of something. If nothing else, she could always play the "lost, lonely waif" role again.

The grandmotherly African-American woman in front of her turned around. "Would you like some gum, sweetheart?" She held out a pack of Doublemint, one shiny silver rectangle extended for her to grasp.

Cindy had an impulse to tell the woman she couldn't take candy from strangers, but didn't really want to do anything that helped people remember her. To escape, she needed to be invisible, so anyone who asked after her wouldn't be able to follow far. So, she thanked the woman and popped the gum into her mouth, surprised by the rich, sweet flavor. Her stomach growled.

The woman laughed. "Goodness. Did you miss your supper tonight?"

Trying for a nonthreatening charm, Cindy smiled. She'd been good at that once and could learn to use what advantages she had again. "I'm afraid so. It's been quite a day!"

"I'd say. Your clothes are a mess, dear."

Cindy looked down. Her baggy pants were grass stained from her struggle on the lawn. Her shirt bloused around her skinny frame, but didn't hide its torn edges. One of her sneakers flapped, gap-mouthed, the sole disconnected from the rest of the shoe. She ran her hands over her head self-consciously and found her hair sticking up at odd angles, too. The woman must imagine her a runaway. Why else would a kid her apparent age be out alone?

"We had a field trip today, and I stayed late at my friend's house by campus. My mom is going to be angry about these pants."

The woman relaxed a little at the mention of Cindy's mother. And it wasn't a lie. Her mother would have been upset about the state of her clothes—if she were still alive to notice such things.

"Nothing a little Spray-n-Wash won't take out, I suppose. That bruise though..." The woman pointed at Cindy's cheek.

Cindy touched the spot tenderly and found it swollen and sore. She'd almost forgotten Patricia had punched her. Now she'd have to convince this stranger she wasn't a victim of abuse. The last thing she needed would be to get off the bus and find child services waiting to take her into protective custody.

She laughed again, trying to pitch the sound high and affect a carefree, shrugging attitude. "I know! It's a beaut, isn't it? I took a spill off Patty's trampoline and caught the frame with my face on the way down. I'm just glad I didn't knock out another tooth. Mom really would be pissed then."

The woman looked at her sharply.

Shit, maybe "pissed" isn't right. Do kids say pissed?

Cindy held her gaze, remembering to blink steadily. Not blinking revealed a lie as easily as blinking too much. She had to strike the right balance.

The woman knew the power of silence, though. It stretched long between them, while her dark eyes locked on those bruises. Cindy's mind raced to add to her story, make the lady accept it and move on. Could she say something to make her think this was cultural, a Chinese thing? Probably not. She tried not to fidget or look askance.

Luckily for her, a ping sounded, followed by a recorded voice announcing the stop for Morris Square. The lady gathered her belongings and pulled the cord to show she wanted off.

Cindy sagged with relief.

As she stood to leave, the woman handed her a candy bar and a business card. "I hope everything really is all right, sweetheart. But if it isn't, you call me. We can help."

Cindy didn't say anything as the woman walked away. She kept her eyes on the floor, automatically counting the tread lines and noticing the break in the pattern where a patch had been applied. Only after the bus started moving again did she read the purple and gold card. The woman was a social worker. That had been close.

Sliding into the darker corner near the window, Cindy sprawled her gangly legs across the rest of the seat to discourage anyone who might try to sit near her. She wished she had some headphones or a phone to play with, something to send out the signal she didn't want to interact with anyone.

The gemstones in her pocket bit into her hipbones. She found it comforting, knowing they hadn't been lost. Her head fell against the seat and Cindy closed her eyes. She didn't have to pretend to be tired. She wasn't used to this kind of running around. What she wouldn't give for a quiet day behind her microscope again, uncovering secrets instead of living them. The journey would be long and she didn't even know yet where she'd go.

2

PATRICIA PICKS UP THE PIECES

M a'am?" A young man in a dark blue jumpsuit addressed her. "Ma'am, I need to ask you some questions."

Patricia sighed. Explanation time. She looked down at herself, despairing at the sight. Standing on the street in a ragged sports bra and torn yoga pants, shoeless, scratched, and dirty. Drying blood making her short red hair sticky. Quite a vision of loveliness. Cindy had just gotten away on the bus that had driven off minutes earlier. She wanted nothing more than to chase it down the road, but she'd never be able to catch it. She was spent, and not to mention, too old for this shit. Would this guy buy "senior moment" as a reason for her appearance?

The campus quad behind her still burned in places, and a line of emergency vehicles blocked half the street.

Emergency vehicles.

Jessica.

She grasped the man's arm. "Are you an EMT?" Not giving him time to answer, she dragged him along as she ran back to the quad. "Come with me!"

A group of people already worked over Jessica Roark, and Patricia dropped to her knees. Maybe they could save her, the stupid brave fool. She watched, flooded by guilt, worry, disgust and fear all at once. The thousand needlepoint itch of her scales trying to emerge swept over her cheeks and arms and she gulped huge gasps of air trying to find the focus to bring them back in. It wasn't working. Ragged emerald plates pushed out from the flesh on her arms. The struggle to control her transformation left her dizzy and nauseated. Her body heaved and she scrambled for the bushes, emptying the contents of her stomach in three long retches. She needed to get it together. Flopping back onto her bottom in the grass, she drew in long, slow breaths and felt her scales retract.

The young man in the blue jumpsuit walked up to her again. "Ma'am, do you need medical attention?"

Patricia shook her head weakly, hoping the shadows hid her well enough as she pulled in her scales. Exhaustion made them hard to control. It wasn't the smooth, fast trick she thought she had mastered, but an awkward and uneven action, like voluntarily sticking herself with splinters. She eventually succeeded and risked an evaluative look at the man so determined to talk to her.

The man's face remained impassive. She couldn't tell what he had seen or what he thought of it. "Where..." she started to ask, but reconsidered. She didn't know what had happened to Leonel, or Suzie, or Eva. And she didn't want to be the one to start passing out names and information to the authorities.

"Your friends are all safe," he told her.

That's what you think.

Safe wasn't a word she would apply to any of them. Not anymore. Not since the change altered all of them in unheard of ways.

The man crouched in front of her and held out a bottle of water. Patricia took it and downed half in one swallow. He wasn't as young as she thought at first. He looked to be in his mid-forties, maybe even a bit older. Handsome, too, in that chiseled jaw and broad shoulders sort of way. The fitness of his body had fooled her. Most men anywhere near her age couldn't maintain that kind of shape anymore. This one had a military haircut, but his blue jumpsuit didn't sport a nametag or insignia of any sort. He also had yet to identify himself. She finished the water, crushed the bottle, and gave it back to him.

He stood and held out a hand to her. She grasped his arm at the elbow and let him pull her to her feet, wobbling a little.

"Are you sure about the medical care? We should get you checked out." He guided her back toward the center of the quad.

She didn't pull away from the support he offered. A few steps away, Jessica lay on a transport bed, a clear liquid IV bag hanging above her as two blue jump-suited women pushed her stretcher between them. Eva jogged alongside as the EMTs approached the ambulance, one hand on her daughter's abdomen. Whether out of love or to keep her from floating away, Patricia couldn't have said. At least Jessica had her mother and doctors. If she'd gotten that girl killed, she'd never forgive herself.

"Patricia!" The high, clear shout carried over the other noise.

Patricia and her escort stopped and scanned the area. She hadn't yet spotted Suzie when the young blonde intern bounded into her with a surprisingly strong hug. "Thank God you're all right."

Patricia held her at arm's length, grimacing a little. The fight had left her bruised and aching, making Suzie's embrace as uncomfortable as it was welcome. Suzie looked mostly unscathed. Her light blonde hair was even still coifed.

"What about you? Are you hurt?" Patricia wanted the reassurance verbally, unwilling to trust her eyes.

Suzie held out an elbow wrapped in a clean white bandage, above which her blouse had been torn and neatly tucked. "Just a bad scrape. I bumped my head, too, but they say I don't have a concussion. Jessica, she…" The rest dissolved in a sob Suzie did her best to quell. Her lip shook, but she wiped away tears and steadied herself.

The man in the blue jumpsuit cleared his throat, reminding them of his presence. "Our team is already en route to the burn unit with Ms. Roark. I assure you she'll get excellent care, the very best there is. Let's get you checked out, Ms. O'Neill."

Patricia blinked away the shock of hearing the man use her name.

She hadn't identified herself. She tried to catch Suzie's eyes, but the younger woman's attention remained on Eva and Jessica.

The man let go of Patricia's arm and led the two women to a small tent on the lawn, in front of the wall where she and Leonel had taken down Helen. Though suspicious, she decided to cooperate. For now. She could always transform if following turned out to be a bad idea.

Before ducking her head to enter, she looked at the building again. Helen was nowhere to be seen, though scorched earth and destroyed shrubberies marked the battle scene. The emergency crews must have already removed the body. Patricia was glad. She didn't think she could have faced that now. Even in self-defense, death would leave a dark mark on her soul.

She sank into the chair Suzie led her to and cooperated with a young female medic's attentions, extending her arm while holding and releasing breaths as instructed. The woman removed her stethoscope from her ears and smiled at Patricia, then stood to report to the man in the blue jumpsuit.

"She's all right, sir. Dehydrated, some bruises and scrapes, but no serious injuries. In rather amazing shape for her age." Catching herself in the middle of what might have been a salute, she instead inclined her head and slipped out the flap of the tent. Patricia grimaced at Suzie. "For her age" stung a bit.

The man pulled up a chair in front of her, turning it backward so he could rest his muscular forearms on the seat back as he straddled it. "Ms. O'Neill? We'll get you to that rest as soon as we can, but I really need to ask you some questions now."

Suzie stood, cell phone at the ready. "Should I contact your lawyer, Patricia?"

The man spread his hands wide. "If you want a lawyer here, that is certainly your right, but you're not being arrested or accused of any crime, Ms. O'Neill. I'm not even a police officer. We've kept them out of this."

Patricia raised an eyebrow at the man. A dull ache announced a probable black eye. She wondered when that had happened and how.

Her skin was nigh-indestructible when she let her lizard self out. "We?"

He grinned, revealing a mouth full of model-perfect teeth that made him look more like an actor playing a soldier than a real one. "Yes, ma'am. We. The Department."

3

CINDY JUMPS FROM THE FRYING PAN

Someone shook her shoulder. "Miss?"

Cindy jumped, panicked and alert.

"Miss, we're at the station. End of the line. Do you need help finding your connection?"

Cindy recovered herself and tried to sound confident; a capable and trustworthy child. She let her hair fall forward to keep the driver from focusing on the swelling bruise on her cheek. The tight flesh ached when she swallowed. It had definitely gotten worse while she slept. "It's okay. My father is meeting me."

Worry dropped off the man's face. "That's good. I'd be concerned about you out here alone."

Cindy managed not to roll her eyes at the paternalistic attitude. Better to let him see a docile child rather than a belligerent teenager. "I won't be alone long." She slid past him into the aisle and patted her pockets as she exited the bus. The gems and her wallet still nestled in the too-loose pants sliding down her narrow hips. It would be enough to get started. The real question was where to go from here.

Her house had been destroyed in the fire, along with her laboratory, thanks to Helen's overzealous defense. Helen had loved her new fire-wielding abilities a little too much, and while Cindy appreciated the support, she wished her new friend hadn't destroyed everything in the process. All that remained of her work was what she'd uploaded to her secured backup servers. That, and what she had in her mind. Time pressed on her. She needed a reliable lab and the sooner, the better. Without more serum, she didn't know what might happen.

When Cindy left the bus, she walked directly to a point on the sidewalk outside the station, her speed and sense of purpose completing the illusion she would meet someone there. She paced a few minutes, impatiently, until two buses moved behind her. Figuring the commotion would mask her departure, she ran into the station proper and found an ATM. She popped all the cards in the wallet in one after another and withdrew the maximum amount of cash allowed, sliding the bills into her pockets. She kept checking her surroundings. No one seemed to be paying attention to her.

Next, she'd have to get out of Springfield. Patricia and her foolish busybody "friends" wouldn't leave her unmolested long. Though it was amusing to imagine them trying to explain the truth to the police, Patricia would find something plausible to tell the authorities, and soon, Cindy would be dodging nosy officials of one sort or another. It would be better to get some miles between herself and this town before the hammer came down. She read the station's marquee listing the possible destinations and considered. She had connections in many of these cities, but none she could rely on fully. No one like Patricia had once been. But that bridge lay in ashes now, quite literally burned. If she and her oldest friend ever met again, it wouldn't be for coffee and doughnuts.

Cindy had no family to speak of. Her father died when she was just a toddler, her mother more recently. If she had any aunts or uncles or cousins, she knew nothing about them. Her colleagues, those she hadn't already alienated, wouldn't know her in this new, youthful body. The best friend she'd ever had, her only friend, was beyond her reach now. It might be lonely but solitude would keep her safe and involve less risk than getting help from others. At least if she relied on only herself, she knew exactly who she'd be dealing with.

"Cindy?"

She turned automatically at the sound of her name, then wished she could take it back. So much for playing it cool. The man who had spoken looked about a hundred years old, almost mummified inside the loose wrinkles around his narrow face. He wore a long jacket despite the heat of the spring day, the kind easy to hide something inside. His bright, piercing blue eyes examined her with avid interest.

"It is you. Wow. He wasn't kidding, was he?"

"Listen, I don't know who you are or who you think I am, mister, but you need to leave me alone or I'm going to scream for help." Cindy backed away, trying to keep an eye on the man and choose a direction to run at the same time. This man knew her name and she didn't have the faintest idea who he was or what he wanted.

"Calm down, little lady," he said. "We're not here to hurt you."

A cold, hard thing pressed against her ribs. She startled at the sudden contact and looked back and up into the smiling face of a younger man, maybe thirty or thirty-five, dark-skinned and muscular.

"Just do as you're told." He pushed her toward the old man.

"We'll explain in the car." The old man led the way, his coat swishing behind him.

Cindy stumbled down the sidewalk, her head on a swivel. Her panic must have been visible on her face, but she couldn't seem to make eye contact with anyone. All the other travelers, busy with their own concerns, failed to notice her. Most didn't even glance in her direction. She'd gotten her wish to become invisible, right when she needed to be seen.

She considered making a break for it. These men probably thought they could rule her by fear alone. They might not be prepared for her to duck and run. Cindy peered back at the man behind her, his gun in her ribs. Tall and fit, with bright eyes that showed an active mind. She analyzed him, calling on her training in *mien xiang,* face reading. The resolution of his jawline spoke of a willingness to act decisively. His association with the Chinese element of metal signified a man who believed himself righteous in his cause. Cindy quailed at the idea of him chasing her in the bus station. She'd never been much of an athlete and could easily envision him catching her and throwing her down like an escaped dog.

A black limousine waited at the curb. The old man walked around and seated himself in the front passenger seat. A man in a traditional chauffeur's uniform held the back door open.

"Ms. Liu." He bowed slightly and gestured for her to enter. He pronounced her name correctly in Chinese, with two syllables and a decidedly un-American vowel sound.

Unable to think of anything else to do, Cindy obeyed, scooting to the other side of the seat as the armed man slid in beside her, his bulk pressing her nearer the door. The door closed, and within another moment or two, the car maneuvered into traffic and sped down the road.

Cindy wrapped her arms around herself, making and rejecting plans like her brain channel-surfed a TV in her mind.

"Are you cold, dear?" The voice came from the darkened corner of the opposite seat. It sounded like sandpaper rubbed over something damp and sent a fresh chill down her spine. She shook slightly. "Davis, give her your jacket."

The gunman grunted his disapproval, but did as he'd been told, shrugging out of his jacket and passing it to Cindy. She draped it across her shoulders, feeling even smaller inside the giant man's clothing. Peering into the corner the voice had come from, she made out the general shape of a man in the shadows.

"Who are you? What do you want with me?" She didn't like the warble in her voice. It made her sound weak.

A wheeze preceded a cough and an odd barking noise. Was that laughter? She turned a sidelong glance at Davis, who fiddled with his phone, avoiding eye contact.

"You are forthright. Just like your mother."

"What do you know about my mother?" Cindy's senses went on full alert now. These people knew her name and claimed to know her mother. She snaked her hand toward the door under the jacket, trying to prep herself to roll out when the car stopped again. She didn't like her chances of surviving such a maneuver, but she liked her chances trapped in a car with armed strangers even less.

"You look like her. She had that same stubborn, pointed chin, and laser-sharp eyes."

Cindy glared at him. "Are you going to tell me how much I've grown since you saw me last, too?"

That wheezing laughter again. It sounded like an asthmatic fit. "On the contrary. In fact, I think you may have gotten smaller. Weren't you five feet tall before you started your treatments? And at least a stone heavier?"

Cindy let go of the door handle and stared at the shadowy man. "Who are you?"

"Haven't you guessed?" The man leaned forward, his hands resting on a cane held between his knees. She scanned his face, from the pale freckled skin and round glasses, to the obvious dark-circles under his eyes and the way the skin bunched up around his ears. European descent, probably in his early forties, a complete stranger to her. She shook her head.

The man smiled, a slow gesture that twitched as it formed, a hitch in the motion. "I'm your father."

4

PATRICIA GETS A JOB OFFER

D epartment of what?"

"Just the Department."

Patricia looked at Suzie, who looked back at her, cell phone still at the ready to call the lawyer. She winked at her intern and looked back to the man in front of them. "Mister...?"

"Austin."

"Mr. Austin, I'm fifty-eight. That makes me too old for pussyfooting around and playing games. Let's get to the point, shall we?"

A smile of real enjoyment spread across the man's face. He flashed those perfect teeth again. "Gladly. I'm Lucas Austin, recruiter for the Department, and we want you to come work for us."

"This is a job interview?" Patricia almost laughed aloud.

"No ma'am. This is a job offer." He pulled back the tent flap, revealing the wall of the building behind them and the distinct shape of human body embedded in the broken brickwork. "That was the interview."

Suzie stepped in front of the flap, blocking Patricia's view of the damage. She pulled a business card out of her small blue pocketbook and proffered it to Austin, who took it, surprise evident on his face. "Mr. Austin, as you can plainly see, Ms. O'Neill has been through quite an ordeal today. She needs a shower and rest. If you contact me at that number, we can schedule an appointment to discuss your offer." She turned to Patricia. "Are you ready, Ms. O'Neill?"

Patricia stood, grabbed another bottle of water from the table, and followed her assistant out the flap and down the path to the parking lot, strutting a little despite her bare feet and ruined pants. No one tried to stop them and Patricia didn't look back.

S uzie turned the key and her Honda Civic started, blaring pop music. She clicked off the stereo and looked expectantly at her employer.

Patricia realized she was waiting for instructions. "Was that Katy Perry?"

Suzie nodded, a smile tugging at the corners of her small pink lips.

"Turn it back on and take me home," said Patricia, finding the handle to lower the seat into a reclined position. Sometimes music made it easier to think.

They didn't talk as Suzie drove. Patricia watched the treetops whizzing past, not even trying to control her whirling thoughts. Out there, somewhere, Cindy rode the bus away from capture. Jessica had been taken to the hospital. Helen might be dead. Her mind replayed one particular scene in graphic detail.

"Trust me," Leonel had yelled, and she'd given him her hand. He'd flung her at Helen. The thick sound of her claw making contact with Helen's jaw reverberated in her mind. The woman's body seemed to turn to jelly as she crumpled to the ground, one hand still ablaze with the fireball she'd summoned to throw at them. Leonel purpled with rage as he picked Helen up and threw her against the wall with all his considerable strength, his handsome face distorted into something monstrous. Helen's limbs bent at angles that defied the body's geometry. It didn't matter that she'd attacked them first. They had broken her.

She sat up, startled, and yelled, "Leonel!"

Suzie swerved onto the rumble strip in the shoulder, cursed softly, and righted the car. "You scared the crap out of me, Patricia!"

Patricia stared at her. "After all we've been through today, my yelling scared you?"

"I thought you were asleep."

"Where's Leonel?"

"He was talking with another one of the blue jumpsuit guys. Do you want me to go back for him?" She scanned the beltway ahead, probably looking for an exit.

"Give me your phone."

Suzie gestured at the center console with her head and Patricia picked up the phone in its bright pink case. After Suzie told her the unlock code, Patricia called Leonel, but it went to voicemail. She hung up and redialed, but it went to voicemail again. While she tried to decide what she could leave as a message, the phone rang. "Hello?"

"Who is this?" A man's voice—not Leonel, so she guessed it must be his husband, David.

"Patricia."

The man called out to someone, his voice muffled like he had covered the microphone, "*Es Patricia. Quieres hablar con ella?*" He returned, sounding hard and angry, but also worried. "My wife doesn't want to talk to you right now. She said to tell you she's fine and she'll call you tomorrow." He hung up.

Patricia stared at the phone for a minute before she locked it and put it back. Leonel had only recently become a man, but hearing him referred to as "my wife" boggled the mind. In any case, the Alvarez family didn't want her around right now.

"Do I need to turn around?"

"No. Let's just go home." She stayed upright for the rest of the journey, staring out the window and trying to sort out how she felt and what she should do next.

5

CINDY IS TAKEN FOR A RIDE

My father?" Now it was Cindy's turn to laugh. She brayed merrily, warranting an ugly look from Davis, the body-guard. She was tempted to spit on the floor, like the very idea necessitated protections against a curse. "My father is dead."

The man nodded. "That's what you were told. Evangeline never knew any differently. It was for her safety, and yours."

The use of her mother's name quieted Cindy. It didn't mean the man's story was true, but it meant he had personal information about her. Clearly, this man could not be her father. For one thing, he was far too young. In spite of the walking stick and signs of ill health, the man looked forty-five at the oldest. He also looked more Irish than Hungarian. Angry at herself for even considering his claims, Cindy threw out her arms, the quick motion making the bodyguard tense for action.

"Am I supposed to be impressed that you know her name? Wow. Guess even an old guy like you can use Google, huh?"

"You're no spring chicken yourself, young lady." Heavy emphasis on the word "young" raised the hairs on the back of her neck and earned a sideways look from Davis, his hand still resting on his holstered gun. Cindy pushed out her lower lip, knowing it made her look even more like a petulant child. She'd play her part as long as she could.

The man rested his cane on the seat beside him and slid over so they sat face-to-face and knee-to-knee. She caught a whiff of something sour, like old butter or half-rotten meat, and wrinkled her nose.

"You may look the part, Cindy Liu, but I was there when you were born, sixty-seven years ago. You aren't the child you seem to be. What I want to know is how you did it."

Oh, was that it?

He wanted the formula.

She should've expected this. Even with all her precautions, the secret couldn't remain hidden forever, and when the scientific world learned what she'd been able to do, she'd have more attention than she wanted. "So, if you know that, then you'd know my father, were he living, would be nearly one hundred years old. I must say, you're holding up well, all things considered."

He leaned back in his seat, smiling again, that slow, hitching slide. "You yourself are evidence that you can't always judge a book by its cover, my dear. This," he gestured at his own visage and body, "is not my original skin."

Cindy felt her eyes grow wide despite her best attempts to keep a poker face. Then her natural skepticism rose to the surface. She crossed her arms again. "Convince me."

"When I knew your mother, my name was Anton Lorre. She was an assistant in my lab. And I—"

"Abused your position and sexually harassed your employee?"

He barked a harsh laugh. "Yes, something like that, I suppose. Evangeline might have seen it that way. I take it she didn't speak highly of me?"

Cindy shrugged. She'd been conned before. She wouldn't feed him any details to upholster the furniture of his lies.

"Project Osiris was about longevity," continued the old man, "about extending a man's interval on Earth, gaining him more time to develop his ideas and do his work."

Cindy yawned, not bothering to cover her mouth.

He stopped talking, seeming to study her instead.

She returned his gaze with a flat stare.

A spasm moved across the left side of his face and he turned his head away from her, visibly bracing himself as it passed.

Cindy and the bodyguard exchanged a look. Davis didn't seem to know what to make of the spasm, either.

The tremor under control, he continued. "As I said, your mother was an assistant in my lab. We became lovers." He looked up sharply as he said this, as if Cindy might be shocked by such talk. "You were born on a rainy night in April of 1946. Your mother didn't call me. She had already decided she didn't want me in your lives by then. But I came anyway. Fathers were not allowed in the birthing area back then, and your mother refused to see me afterward, but she couldn't keep me from seeing you." He went silent for a long moment, sighed, and went on. "I never wanted to be a father, but there's something to be said for the biological imperative. I always kept track of you, tried to help any way I could."

Cindy guessed she was supposed to feel touched by his interest, but she already knew this story from the other side—the side where she grew up lonely, listening to her embittered mother rail against her father on the rare occasions she mentioned him at all. Nothing in this tale convinced her that the slight, brown-haired man seated across from her was her father. Even if he told the truth, he'd given up his claim on his daughter readily enough, and now, he only wanted her research. That made him as much a predator as any stranger. "Very moving. Maybe you can sell the story to Lifetime. I hear they eat up that kind of garbage."

Another tremor crossed the man's face, but this time Cindy recognized it as anger and not palsy. He picked up his cane and tapped the glass behind his head with the silver handle. A window rolled down, and the old man who had accosted her on the sidewalk looked back.

"Bertrand, the envelope, please."

He nodded and passed back a manila envelope.

The man claiming to be Cindy's father handed it to the bodyguard, who opened it and passed it back to him. He pulled out an old photograph and handed it to Cindy.

Brown, as old photographs become when not well preserved, the paper had softened around the edges. A crease crossed the bottom where it must have been bent and flattened again. It made a white line across the skirt of the woman in the picture: her mother. Beautiful in a way Cindy remembered seeing only rarely, Evangeline Liu wore a simple dark dress with a lace collar and smiled up at a man, her face framed by a stylish hat. The man looked into the camera, and Cindy didn't like his smug expression or the hand on her mother's waist, gripping tightly enough to pull the skirt askew and reveal the lace of her slip. But she knew the visage. Her father. She turned it over and recognized her mother's handwriting, small and neat and clear: "San Francisco, 1945. Anton and Evangeline." Uncharacteristically, she'd drawn a small heart beneath their names.

She handed the photograph back to the man. "A nice bit of history, but this," she tapped the tall, dark-haired man in the photograph and looked meaningfully at the shorter, lighter-haired, freckled man in front of her, "is obviously not you."

"Ah, yes. Well, it is, and it isn't. It's complicated."

"I'm in no hurry."

The car stopped. "It'll be easier to show you. Come. We have a plane to catch."

6

PATRICIA COMES CLEAN

A half-hour shower and a long nap later, Patricia felt like a new woman. One a lot cleaner and less scaly than the woman Suzie had driven home. When she woke, she padded out to the living room dressed in drawstring pajama pants and an ancient tee shirt from her college days. She found Suzie asleep on the sofa, her laptop open and papers spread out on the coffee table in front of her. Leaving her intern to rest, she went to the kitchen to find a menu and order Chinese food. Given that the last time Suzie had gone for food, she had ended up needing a rescue from a giant fireball, they'd use delivery this time.

No notifications on her phone. No messages. She called Leonel, but it went straight to voicemail again. Jessica's mother's phone number wasn't in her contacts and Patricia didn't know if Eva would talk to her anyway. Not after her half-assed plan to capture Cindy and make her talk had gotten them all into this mess. If they blamed her for Jessica's burns and the turmoil of their lives, they could get in line to beat her up, right behind Patricia herself.

Patricia had insisted they could capture Cindy Liu themselves, rather than begging help from any authorities. At the time, she would've said she was protecting the police from a situation they weren't equipped to handle, but the truth involved a more compli-cated blend of desire for personal vengeance and her long friendship with Cindy. She'd been so sure Cindy would talk to her, if she could've gotten her alone. Instead, the little bitch had stolen her phone and called Helen, resulting in the firefight that nearly killed them all. And after everything, she'd gotten away.

Patricia wished she knew what Leonel had said to these Depart-ment people, whoever they were. She wanted to send some kind of authorities after Cindy, but didn't know how to tell their story to law enforcement. They'd think her crazy. After all, she'd been there for all of it and even *she* thought it sounded crazy.

She imagined the scene. "No, really, officer. That tween over there is actually sixty-seven years old. She's been experimenting on herself and all of us, that's why she looks like a child. The woman you found dead on campus could throw fire. This man over here used to be a woman. Careful, he's stronger than he looks. That little blonde can fly. And me, well, let me show you." At best, it would end with the EMTs working over the body of the officer after his heart attack. More likely, they'd all end up in a lab somewhere being studied.

The doorbell rang. She picked up her wallet and hurried to answer, calling to Suzie that it was all right. She opened the door, two twenties in her hand. The usual teenager from the Chinese restaurant waited on the stoop, and behind him stood Lucas Austin, no longer wearing the blue jumpsuit, but somehow still looking official in jeans and a white button-up shirt.

He handed the delivery boy a fifty-dollar bill. "I've got this. Keep the change, kid."

Patricia knew the kid wasn't supposed to take anything bigger than a twenty, but he snatched the money and high-tailed it back to his little red car with the white plastic bubble on top advertising the restaurant.

Suzie appeared behind Patricia in the doorway and reached for the food. "I asked you to call for an appointment, Mr. Austin." She stalked off toward the dining room table.

"You might as well come in," said Patricia. For fun, she turned her eyes reptilian as he walked past her.

He blinked. "Thank you. And please call me Lucas."

Patricia and Lucas sat at the table eying each other warily until Suzie reappeared with bowls and glasses and busied herself opening containers. The intern cleared her throat. "So, I've been looking into the Department. There seems to be some disagreement as to what you folks do, and who you work for, or whether you even exist."

"I assure you we do indeed exist." He accepted a bowl and filled it with lo mein noodles.

Hungry, Patricia plowed into her food without concern for the stranger at the table. She shoveled sesame chicken, moo goo gai pan, egg rolls, and potstickers in her mouth while Suzie gave Lucas the third degree.

Lucas kept his cool as he fielded her questions, clearly used to incredulous and suspicious reactions in his line of work.

The short version: the Department was a secret organization that specialized in unusual cases.

"Think X-Files without aliens, at least so far," he said, chuckling at his own joke.

"Not interested." Patricia reached for the last egg roll.

"You haven't heard my offer yet."

"At this point in my life, sonny, I make the offers. I'm not interested in working for the government."

"I'm sorry to hear that." The man seemed like he might genuinely be sorry. "We do good work. I hate to see you pass up a chance to be part of something so exciting, something that can really utilize your special skills."

Patricia looked pointedly at Suzie, who stood to see the man to the door. "Thank you for your kind offer, Mr. Austin, but Ms. O'Neill is not interested at this time."

Austin stood, holding his hands to the side in a gesture of surrender. "All right, I'll go. You know how to find me if you change your mind." He left a business card on the table. It lacked any logo or words, featuring only a phone number.

As soon as the door closed behind him, Suzie hurried back to the table. "Why don't you even want to hear what he has to say?"

"Please. 'Utilize my special skills.' He might as well have come out and said they planned to exploit me for their own ends. I'll steer my own ship, thanks."

"But, Patricia, they've got to have resources we could tap to find Cindy."

"Probably. But we're pretty resourceful ourselves. Some kinds of help are more trouble than they're worth."

7

WHO'S YOUR DADDY, CINDY LIU?

During the plane ride, Cindy examined the envelope of documents she'd been handed. It made for interesting reading. The small private plane meant no security checkpoint or even additional staff. The chauffeur piloted. She sat alone in one area, while the man who claimed to be her father sat closer to the cockpit with Bertrand and Davis, the handsome gunman who had picked her up at the bus station. The three men murmured, their words hard to make out over the noise of the engines.

She caught snippets of the conversation. They seemed concerned about some upcoming deadline, argued about funding, staffing, and downscaling. That made dear old Daddy angry. He blustered about how science shouldn't depend on the judgment of fools to justify its existence.

"Aren't I proof of my own theories? What more do they need?"

The bodyguard caught her peering around her seat. He shook his head and gestured that she should turn around. It pissed her off, but she complied. Her curiosity piqued, she wanted to stay close until she understood.

The contents of the envelope kindled her interest, too. The documents described Project Osiris, a between-the-wars experiment, which tried to transfer consciousness from one body to another, promising to let "the best and brightest minds extend their lives beyond the limits of the human body." Regardless whether the man sitting in the other section of this plane was who he claimed to be or not, her father had evidently been involved in the project.

In 1948, the year she believed to have been his last, Anton Lorre had signed a contract making himself a human test subject. Financial documents detailed payments to Evangeline Liu in the exact amount Cindy remembered from her childhood as her mother's pension. The fellowship that paid for Cindy's first degree appeared to have been created expressly for her. Project Osiris had lurked in the shadows of her entire life, removing small obstacles and providing opportunities. Even Dr. Victor Chaney, the man who had helped cryogenically freeze Cindy's fiancé in the 1980s had been tied to the project.

She flipped through the documents again and again, spotting new connections each time. Eventually, she tossed the folder on the empty seat beside her and stared out the window, fingering the photograph of her mother and Anton Lorre. Her reflection looked back at her, appearing all of thirteen years old. It wasn't inconceivable that the man was telling the truth. Her own work provided evidence that the limits of science had not yet been reached. But did she want to ally herself with these people? What exactly did they want from her? The formula for her youth serum, obviously. But was there more to it than that?

It looked like she might get an answer.

Anton Lorre, or whatever he called himself in this skin, maneuvered down the aisle towards her, his cane tapping as he moved. Cindy watched him, getting the impression he was off-balance. One of his legs dragged. She remembered the odd twitching hitch in his facial expressions and the tremor that had overtaken his face in the car and wondered if the man had a neurological condition or had recently suffered a stroke.

He flopped into the seat across from hers with an audible groan. "Are you convinced?"

Cindy picked up the envelope and shook its contents straight. "I'm convinced my father was involved in some shady experiments, but there's nothing here to convince me that you are him."

He nodded, more times than necessary, almost like he couldn't stop the motion once he started it. "Bertrand thought you might need more convincing. Here." He handed her a pair of earbuds and a tablet computer, then reached across to unlock it for her, an odor of something like mothballs drifting from his skin, which looked gray in the over-seat lighting. Cindy wondered again at the exact nature of his health issues. "They've digitized the old films. We still have about an hour left in our flight. That should be enough time to let you watch some of them."

Cindy scrolled through the videos, each labeled with a date and two names. The first was 1948-Lorre-Carradine. She paused, her finger over the icon. "Why do you care if I believe you? You've already got me here, taking me wherever you're taking me. Why does it matter if I believe you?"

"I want you on my side, Cindy. And I think you will be after you see these videos. We can be of use to each other."

Pushing off, he swayed back up onto his feet and worked his way down the aisle. When he settled back in his seat, the bodyguard-gunman pulled out a silver case and removed a syringe from it. "Your arm, Mr. Price."

Her alleged father cooperated, removing his jacket and rolling up his sleeve to reveal mottled flesh, discolored purple and yellow like a healing bruise. After receiving the injection, he leaned back and seemed to go to sleep.

Cindy turned her attention to the videos, mentally filing away the name she'd heard. Mr. Price. She slipped an earbud in and clicked the first one.

Two men sat by side on a lab table, dressed in hospital gowns.

"I am Anton Lorre," said the first. Cindy knew his face from the few pictures her mother had not destroyed, the ones she kept in the false bottom of her lingerie drawer along with the other things she didn't want her daughter to see. She recognized his hooded brow and dark eyes, even with his head shaved bald of his dark, oily locks. She barely glanced at the other man who introduced himself as Max Carradine in a clipped British accent. The two men gave a brief explanation of the process. They planned to transplant Anton's brain into Max's body and Max's brain into some kind of stasis. The plan sounded insane, but both men spoke with enthusiasm, confident it would work.

Cindy skimmed the footage of the actual procedure. It turned her stomach. Surgery, so far as she was concerned, endured as the most barbarous aspect of western medicine. Reliance on cutting pieces of a person out or off and calling it a cure weighed heavily in her decision not to become a western doctor. The body could be brought back into balance so many other ways if the physician remained open to all possibilities.

She clicked on next video, labeled "Post-op." This time, Max Carradine sat alone on the table, looking into the camera, the crown of his head ringed by a line of stitches.

"Max didn't make it," the man said slowly, with no trace of the British accent. Cindy couldn't tell if the man's emotions made his speech sloppy or if he had physical trouble forming the words. "The storage technology failed. He's gone." He dropped his head into his hands, gasping horribly. An off-camera voice said that it was all right and they could film this part later. Cindy leaned around to look at the man at the front of the plane. He still slept.

A jump occurred in the film, a splice. Max Carradine appeared again, dressed in a lab coat over regular clothes, hair mostly grown in. His voice and speech patterns were clear now, but definitely not the same as Max's before the procedure.

"It's been an adjustment, being Max, but as you can see, I have gained full motor control." He held out a steady hand, flexed the fingers, and moved the arm to demonstrate. He stood and walked in a circle, the camera following him a little unsteadily as he talked about the strangeness of operating a new body. He pointed out that Max had been left-handed, but the body, now housing Anton's brain, had become right-handed, suggesting the choice lies in the brain. "Our work continues. We learned from the loss of my colleague that the process requires a living host. Thus far, none of our attempts to preserve the brain separate of a body have been successful for more than a few days."

Cindy stopped the video and scanned the list of other files. 1967-Carradine-Rathbone. 1984-Rathbone-Chaney. 2004-Chaney-Price. The bodyguard had called the man he'd injected Price. She clicked that video. Victor Chaney stared out at her from the screen, looking haggard, but recognizably the same man who had preserved her beloved Michael when he lost his fight with cancer. That familiar face among all these strangers chilled her.

Chaney spoke to a web camera, his voice rough. "I'm out of time. I hoped to find another way, not to do this to a friend, but Daniel learned too much. It has to be him. It has to be now." She didn't watch the rest. Strange as it seemed, she hadn't been lying to that bus driver. Her father really had met her at the station.

8

PATRICIA GOES OVER THE HILL

By the next morning, Patricia knew that tracking Cindy wasn't going to be easy without the help of official channels. Your average Jane could only get so much information without connections. Bank information. Missing person reports. Camera footage. Within a few short hours, Patricia's optimism faded into frustration. She'd been so certain her skills would serve her in this scenario.

Eventually, she'd sent Suzie home to get some rest. The poor girl was falling over, but hadn't complained about her exhaustion. Suzie reminded Patricia of her younger self in so many ways. No boundaries. Working ridiculously long hours without consideration of the effects on health and heart. Patricia didn't do that anymore, but she didn't have Suzie's youth either. It wouldn't do any good to tell her. Suzie would have to learn that lesson for herself, like Patricia.

They agreed Suzie would come back for supper, after she took some time to clean up and rest. In the meantime, Patricia would work out a plan. Some next steps.

Moving always helped, so she pulled on some shorts and headed for the park. The running path around the lake had sold Patricia on this condo. Sure, it was a man-made lake, stocked with ornamental fish, but it felt real enough when she ran beside it. The water still smelled like water and the wind still blew through the trees. The roar of cars on the highway invaded the serenity, but she'd learned to ignore that.

Like she always did when she ran, she had a pang for the dog that used to run with her, a golden retriever named, with little kid creativity, Goldie. Goldie had followed Patricia to all her childhood homes, through each stepdad and upheaval. Sometimes Patricia thought that dog had been the only stable thing in her life. She'd loved to run as much as Patricia, and the two of them knew every path in their part of Indiana, including a few they'd made for themselves.

Goldie died right after Patricia left for college, and she had long suspected that her mother had simply failed to take proper care of the animal. Patricia never had another dog after that. She'd been too busy. A dog needed company, and Patricia sometimes didn't come home for weeks at a time at the height of her career. But she still missed Goldie every time she went for a run.

Wanting something difficult, she started with the uphill part of the path. A challenge would distract her enough to let her subconscious work things out. She did her best thinking when she wasn't thinking. Plus, the hilly side usually stayed deserted; most of the other joggers preferred the flatter, easier paths against the water's edge. Pushing herself to do the hill as quickly as possible, she arrived at the top panting and sweaty. Pausing, she bent into a squat to catch her breath. She still felt the effects of her fight in the park the day before. That short run shouldn't have been able to wind her like that. It made her feel old.

A dog whined, a hurt kind of whimper, somewhere close. She jogged along, keeping her step light and trying to zero in on the sound. It grew louder as she approached and voices joined in.

A woman crying. "Please…don't."

She couldn't make out the words, but the other person sounded male and angry. The dog cried again. Patricia picked up her pace.

Around the next curve, she found them. The man pinned the woman to the ground, his hands around her throat. The dog tried to get up. One paw hung askew, obviously broken, and whined as it hobbled towards the woman on the ground. Before she decided what she would do, Patricia dove ahead, unleashing her scaly alter ego. She kicked the man sideways and he fell off the woman onto his side in the dirt, cursing. He started scrambling to his knees, but Patricia didn't give him time to get up. She kicked him in the ribs hard enough that he screamed. The woman sat up and coughed, gasped, and retched. The dog went to her, nosing gently.

Patricia kicked the man again, lifting his body from the ground. He cried out as he curled in on himself, trying to defend against her blows. She let them fly, landing punches and kicks one after another and liking the feeling of his flesh giving under the scaly armor covering her skin. A taste of something metallic and bitter in her mouth fed her anger even more.

She raised her foot to kick the man again, but hesitated at a tug at her elbow. She whirled and found the woman standing, holding herself up against a tree, her face still flushed red. Tears ran down her cheeks silently. She tried to speak, but Patricia couldn't make out the words over the pounding rush of her own blood and breath. It was something soft, though, something like a plea.

Patricia stopped, aghast at how violently she had abused the man gasping at her feet. She could have stopped him with far less. Turning one arm back into ordinary flesh and blood, she picked up the woman's phone from the bushes where it had landed and held it out. "Call for help." She took off running down the path, the torn remnants of her sneakers flapping around her taloned feet.

They covered the incident on the news that night.

Suzie stopped with her forkful of pasta halfway to her mouth and let it fall back on the plate. She grappled for the remote to rewind and turn up the volume.

Patricia didn't meet her eyes as they listened to the details.

"The Lizard Woman of Springfield has been spotted again, this time in the peaceful Lakeside Park area." The camera view changed from the blurry still photo from the time she'd saved the beauty queen at the mall to an overview of the lake, then to footage of a woman being taken away on a stretcher. "Local resident Nancy Feingold had a restraining order against Mark Smith, but that didn't stop him from following her into Lakeside Park when she went to walk her dog this morning."

The screen flashed to a skinny, bleach-blonde woman, her face streaked with tear-ruined makeup, standing in front of the Emergency Room doors. She grabbed the microphone. "Thank God the creature came along when it did. He might have killed my daughter."

Suzie turned the volume down and threw her arm across Patricia's shoulders. "I'm so proud of you!"

Patricia patted Suzie's hand, and tried to feel like she deserved praise, like she was the hero Suzie believed her to be. She had her doubts.

9

CINDY DOES THE TIME WARP AGAIN

Cindy had already decided to accept Price's offer when they arrived. She was short on viable options, and, if nothing else, he provided a means of getting lab equipment and supplies. If she could cash in on her credentials, it would be easy enough to find aid. Many companies would jump to employ a famed researcher like her, even for a brief contract. But, she had to consider her appearance. Who would believe that this seemingly thirteen-year-old girl was actually Dr. Cindy Liu? At least here, she didn't have to worry about proving her identity.

She pulled up the notes app on the tablet and constructed a list of what she needed, including the contact information in China for the emeralds. She'd stabilize her own condition first, then find out what kind of devil she'd made a deal with. Strange times made for strange bedfellows, and these times redefined strange. Her mother had always said Cindy's father was a brilliant, if heartless, man. She guessed she'd find out for herself now.

As they disembarked, Davis appeared at her elbow again. No weapon was visible, but Cindy assumed he had his gun within easy reach and would use it on her if he had cause. She smiled at him brightly, then sashayed up the aisle and down the steps. The pilot-chauffeur had moved to the driver's seat of an SUV. The old man, Bertrand, had taken the front passenger seat again, leaving Cindy with the middle seat, sandwiched between Price and Davis. She crossed her legs to fill as little space as possible, but still felt pinched and trapped between the men.

Twisting a little, she handed the tablet computer to the man she had become convinced was her father. "Here, Pops." She tapped the icon for her supply list. "Can you set up me up with a few things?"

Ignoring her teasing honorific, he took the computer and scanned the list before nodding. "We have everything except the emeralds on hand."

"I'll need more emeralds soon, but I've got a starting supply." She felt her shoulders slide down into place. Knowing she'd be able to make more of the formula soon calmed the worst of her panic. "I want to start immediately." She took back the tablet.

He nodded again. "I understand. And tomorrow, we'll discuss how we can be of use to each other."

Twenty minutes later, Cindy was alone in a lab. Well, alone except for Davis, who sat in the corner watching her. He stayed quiet enough to be practically invisible, though, and she simply pretended he didn't exist. Whatever her doubts about what she'd gotten herself into, she had a shot now. She laid out the supplies, examining the equipment she'd use to fabricate more serum.

The lab was sad, neglected, and a little outdated, but serviceable. It reminded her of the lab she had used as an undergraduate in the 70's, which had seemed impressively modern. Cindy turned on the lights and they flickered a couple of times before staying on, then hummed softly. She sighed, missing the state-of-the-art array in her home lab, controllable from her phone and silent as well as flexible. After a few days in here, her ears would buzz all the time. She tried to be grateful she had a space to work in.

A few hours ago, she hadn't had any idea where she would go or how she would make more of the formula that kept her stable. Now, she had a functional lab to work in, even if she was under guard and owed her probably-insane father a favor in return.

There may have been things she should be grateful for, but starting over like this, here, made her gratitude taste bitter. She had finally had the custom-built lab she always dreamed of in the basement of her mother's old house. Retired, free to sculpt her days any way she chose, to focus her attention on any experiment she wanted. Living near her best friend of forty years for the first time since college. Stunning success with her anti-aging experiments, and unexpected leaps forward with several of her other projects. Then, it had all crashed down around her. Damn Patricia. Damn Jessica. Damn Helen. And damn that man, whoever he was. All that research, lost.

It had seemed such a simple idea. A genetically engineered form of cancer that counteracted the aging process, reactivating senescent cells. Coupled with the serum she'd developed from the emerald powder, her body effectively rejuvenated itself. It worked miraculously well. The results had been immediate and obvious. Within a few weeks, the gray had vanished from her hair and her skin regained some of its former resiliency. Her energy skyrocketed. She felt like a woman half her sixty-seven years.

But it hadn't stopped. Before she knew it, she was dropping years like used tissues until she had the body of a young teen. The time she'd been separated from the emeralds had been devastating. Without treatment, she seemed to get younger by the minute. Yanking at her pants, Cindy cinched the belt tighter and pulled at the bra straps sliding off her shoulders yet again. She peeked down her shirt at the loosely-hanging bra beneath. Her breasts were all but gone. She'd never been curvaceous, but she'd relished her woman's shape and hated this reversion to straight lines and bony limbs. She'd have to put a stop to it.

Once she stabilized her condition and stopped her descent back into childhood, she would hunt them down. All of them. Especially Patricia. If anyone should have understood her work and stood by her side, it was her oldest friend. Patricia had been getting the same push to retire and found it just as offensive. Since when had Patricia gotten so soft that she lost her shit over hazy permissions? Wasn't she an act-now-apologize-later woman? The work meant everything and break-throughs made it all worthwhile. Cindy wouldn't have hurt Jessica. She needed the information hidden in her DNA. All she wanted was to understand. Kidnapping was an ugly word for obtaining study subjects.

But Patricia hadn't understood at all. Instead of supporting her, Patricia had tried to stop her, going so far as to break into her house to steal information, bringing that brute of a man with her, and starting the fight that destroyed her lab. If Cindy hadn't escaped, Patricia would have turned her over to the authorities to waste her genius in a jail cell.

If only Cindy had been able to hold on to Jessica Roark for even a few more days, she would have understood the interaction between the tea and her biology. Of all the people who had sampled the tea, Jessica alone had become airborne. It couldn't be a coincidence she was a cancer survivor. Cindy felt sure that was the key, the reason for such unusual effects. Those butchers had chopped out Jessica's uterus and ovaries like they had carved pieces out of Michael all those years ago. They'd sent poisons through her veins. Perhaps the illness changed the nature of her very cells. If she could understand Jessica's case, she could use what she learned to help herself and maybe even find the key to bringing Michael out of cryo and curing him.

Tomorrow, she'd work on getting back any of her research she could. Though she preferred paper, she had computerized much of her data. There would still be losses. Backups occurred daily, and any data she could recover, she didn't have to try to recreate. The samples were gone, of course. But she might be able to get those again. All she needed was access to the subjects back in Springfield.

First things first, though. She had to take care of herself.

Cindy pulled the remaining fragments of rough emerald out of her pocket and laid them on a cutting surface, running a thumb over the bumpy edges, then rummaged the lab looking for something she could use to cut a sliver. It was probably too much to hope to find a faceter's trim saw, but there had to be something that would work.

Davis looked up from his phone and watched her zip around opening and closing drawers and cabinets after a quick visual inventory. He didn't seem inclined to interfere, so she continued to ignore him.

She almost squealed when she found a small hand-held saw with a diamond blade in a cabinet. Dust covered the device, but it seemed to have all of its pieces. Setting it on the countertop, she found it heavy and difficult to manage now that her hands were even smaller than they used to be, but she'd make it work. After finding some goggles and a hard plastic box she could use to contain the scattering of cut pieces, she set to work.

She broke off two small chunks of the stone, leaving the bulk of the sample intact. It took far less time to find the beakers, burners, and tubing she needed to process the gems into a usable form. She set it all up and looked around for a clock, but didn't find one. Luckily, the tablet had a timer function. Setting it for twenty minutes, Cindy pulled up a stool to stare at her concoction while it bubbled.

As the liquid condensed and dripped into the large beaker at the end, she considered her position. Though he hadn't yet explicitly said it, she understood what her father wanted from her. After body-jumping for decades, he wanted to make the body he had last longer and he thought she could help.

Cindy was less sure.

The nature of her father's experiments twisted her guts when she considered them. She guessed she would have to watch the disgusting surgical videos to better understand the process and identify where it kept going wrong. But the nervous system was a delicate creation, akin to the instruments of an orchestra creating music, and he'd been hacking away at it with electricity and surgical saws. His genius allowed him to make the transfer successfully many times despite the clumsiness of the procedure. She doubted her research could be applied.

Besides, the whole situation gave her pause. Until now, her attitude had been that science amounted to finding out what could be done and doing it. She had yet to find limits that couldn't be overcome with enough perseverance and determination.

Cindy picked up the beaker as the last drop fell inside, and swirled the greenish liquid around, sniffing it. An acrid, pungent smell assaulted her nose, and she turned her head away to avoid coughing into the mixture. It was as it should be. She set it inside a small refrigerator to cool while she went to the medical supply cabinet for a syringe and clean needle

In her work, she had been so focused on the possibilities, she only rarely considered whether it *should* be done. But thinking of her father, the re-animated corpse, she wondered whether it served her best interest to help him. He had left a trail of bodies, like some kind of tornado through the century. But, if she could help, there'd be no further need to kill.

She needed to know more.

After loading the syringe with the barely cooled liquid, she tied off her arm to find a good vein. As she pushed the plunger, she laughed to herself. Yes, she had a lot to learn still. Luckily, thanks to her serum, she had all the time in the world.

10

PATRICIA GETS THE MESSAGE

eonel scolded her in the voicemail. "Why haven't you come
yet? Visiting hours are almost over."
  Patricia groaned and deleted the message.
"Jessica is resting well. We need to talk." Click. Delete.
"This is Leonel. Again. Where are you?" Click. Delete.
Just two words this time. "Call me."
His tone became terser and angrier with each message.
Patricia stared at her phone. She had left it on the table when she'd
gone to bed and hadn't heard any of the calls. She looked at the clock
and decided it was probably too early to call Leonel back now, so she
called the hospital instead to see what they could tell her about Jessica's condition. The visitor relations lady told her that Ms. Roark
would not be having visitors today, but that cards and flowers would
be forwarded to her room. Patricia took the transfer to the gift shop
and ordered an overpriced spring bouquet. It didn't make her feel any
better.

She hadn't considered going to the hospital. Hospital bedsides
were reserved for family. She and Jessica hadn't exactly been friends.
Besides, Jessica's mother wouldn't want her there. If not for her,

maybe Jessica wouldn't have gotten burned. In the same situation, Patricia knew what she'd do, and it wouldn't be pleasant.

Obviously, Leonel disagreed. From the sound of it, he and David had stayed all night and through the next day. Leonel expected Patricia to show up and take a shift, too. She'd have to find a way to make it up to him later.

Today, though, she'd do a little investigation. Sometime during her mostly sleepless night, she'd hit on the idea of tracking Cindy Liu through her credit cards. She bet Cindy hadn't changed her access information since the last time they traveled together.

That last trip to Paris had been their "Forever Young" tour. They shopped and danced and drank their way across the city for nearly two weeks, celebrating Cindy's retirement. They behaved more like college students than women of a certain age. In Paris, no one seemed to find anything shocking or shameful about two older women dancing until three in the morning and taking home men half their ages or younger. It could have been cultural, or maybe their credit card limits were high enough to fly right over censure. Patricia had the best time she'd had in years. She had hoped the two old friends might see the rest of the world over their respective retirements, one trip at a time.

Now it looked like Paris might be her last happy memories from a friendship that spanned most of her adult life. When she found Cindy again, she wouldn't be taking her dancing. Patricia flexed her hand, bringing out the talons and pulling them back in. That woman had things to answer for.

Tapping at the computer didn't satisfy like picking up her old friend and shaking her would, but it was more likely to yield actual answers.

Patricia, according to Cindy, was genetically unable to stop working and relax. "It's your midwestern work ethic," she'd said, half-seriously and half-teasingly. Patricia always brought her laptop along when she traveled. Cindy didn't, but she'd used Patricia's machine when she wanted access to anything, something Patricia pointed out each time it happened. She clicked over to the first of the banking sites. Sure enough, the incautious woman had let the browser save all her login information.

As she'd suspected, Cindy had taken out the maximum cash advance amount on all of her cards on April 17. Had it really only been two days since then? All the withdrawals had been from the ATM at the main bus station at the outskirts of town. No transactions had been made on any of the cards after that, so the money must be holding her over for now. By Patricia's calculations, Cindy had 1500 dollars when she left the bus station. She could've gone anywhere for that. And, if she'd spent cash on her ticket, it would be that much harder to track her.

But not impossible.

Someone would remember a young Asian girl traveling alone.

Patricia put on her favorite pale blue pantsuit and opened the door to head for the bus station. She flung open the door and found Suzie standing there in a bright pink skirt and yellow blouse, hand poised to knock.

Suzie smiled broadly. "I'm glad to see you're ready. Uncle Mike wants to see you. We have an eleven o'clock appointment. That'll give us time to look over this offer." She held up a manila envelope.

Patricia felt her mouth gaping open and snapped it shut. Of all the things she thought she might do today, she hadn't considered going to work, and that wasn't like her. "What day is it?"

"Friday."

That meant it had been a week, almost exactly, since she'd been to the office. A week of her life lost to hunting Cindy Liu. She wouldn't let her former friend ruin her livelihood, too. She picked up her car keys. "I'll drive." As they pulled out of the parking area, she asked what exactly Suzie had told dear old Uncle Mike about why Patricia hadn't been at the office in a week.

Suzie frowned. "I'd gone with 'sick' at first, but that became a problem when you missed so many days in a row, so I went with 'family problems.'"

Patricia snorted. "I bet he was surprised to hear that."

Suzie nodded. "He said he didn't think you had any family."

"Actually, I do, somewhere. But we're not close. We can work with this as a cover story, though. Quick thinking on your part." Patricia parked in front of her favorite breakfast place and Suzie followed her as she walked in, her little heels clicking on the pavement like the claws of her mother's pet Pekingese.

After the waiter poured their coffee and stepped away, Suzie pushed the envelope across the table. "You'd better look at this."

Patricia pulled out the papers and spread them across the table. Suzie sipped her coffee while she pretended to study the art on the walls, giving her time to scan the documents. It didn't take long to figure out what it all meant. "Are they asking me to retire?"

Suzie nodded. "It's not a bad offer."

Patricia let the papers slide to the table. At fifty-eight years old, she had never considered retirement, not in any real sense. She had a portfolio ready, of course, ordinary financial planning. But, actually not working? She drank her coffee, barely noticing when the waiter reappeared with her omelet. She'd been less driven in the past year or so, less engaged by the work. And, if her hours were all her own, she had a much better shot at finding Cindy. The search could be her job instead of an off-hours pursuit. Besides, Suzie would head back to university in a few more weeks for another year in her degree program. No one else at the office would understand.

The sound of her fork sliding on the empty plate a few minutes later startled her.

Suzie watched her intently, her gaze neither pitying nor judging, but merely curious. She'd been there, after all, when Patricia's alter ego had burst out at the office and while she learned to control her transformations. She knew about Cindy and Jessica, Helen and Leonel. If anyone understood why she might want to take this opportunity, it was Suzie.

"What do you think?" the intern asked, a hint of excitement in her voice.

Patricia picked up the proposal and read it over again. Not a bad offer, but they could do better. The incentive to retire early was lower than what they had offered Mr. Carroll a year earlier. "I think they're lowballing me."

Suzie grinned and pulled a laptop out of her bag. "Let's work on a counter offer, shall we?"

11

CINDY'S NEW TOYS

Cindy barreled into the room, slamming the door behind her. Davis jumped from his post in the corner, then relaxed. A hissy fit from his diminutive charge didn't warrant serious action.

Cindy screamed wordlessly. It didn't make her feel better, though it had been satisfying to watch Davis's eyes grow wide.

"I take it he said no?"

She glared at the man. He laughed, which infuriated her all the more. "He said he doesn't have the resources." He'd also said his own research took priority over her "little projects." She was still amazed she hadn't killed him on the spot. Luckily for him, Helen had developed the ability to throw fire, not Cindy.

Davis nodded. "That might be true. This operation is definitely scaled back. If Bertrand weren't still behind the old crackpot, they'd pull the rug out from under him entirely."

It was the most interesting thing the man had said so far. "You think my father is crazy?"

"Don't you?"

Cindy hesitated. She did and she didn't. She understood fully where her father came from. He wanted more time. But the violent path he'd taken to extend his life frightened her. She couldn't approve of his methods, even if she understood his goals.

Davis laughed again and shook his head. "Never mind. You're probably crazy, too. Like father, like daughter." He picked up a magazine and flopped back in his chair, still shaking his head.

Cindy sat, too, pulling her feet up with her and curling her legs so her slender body filled the seat. She thought for a moment, trying to imagine what this whole situation would be like from the outside, to a man like Davis. He wasn't handsome, but she found his face appealing. He had an active intelligence in his eyes and humor in the corners of his mouth.

Something about him reminded her of Michael. Both were black men, Davis and her long-dead fiancé, but their features didn't share much beyond skin color. Davis was tall and broad, while Michael had been shorter and squatter. She decided it came down to attitude. Both sat back and let events unfold in front of them, preserving absolute equanimity in the face of anything that happened. Michael had always tried to get Cindy to adopt his wait-and-see outlook, but she had always been unwilling to leave things to chance when she might be able to affect the outcome.

Davis struck her as a no-nonsense, down-to-Earth sort of man. Practical. Working for her father and learning the details of Project Osiris would seem like insanity to a man like him. But she didn't think it insane to want more time. Didn't everyone? Some people tried to make it happen, while others only idly wished. And sometimes, you had to take drastic measures to get results. More than one brilliant idea had died while waiting for permission. What good would all her efforts to gain more time be if she wasted it waiting?

She jumped up and started gathering materials. Stalling her descent into youth would not be enough. She had to start moving forward again, with or without exactly the right equipment.

A few hours later, she had set up her stations. She spread out her vials and needles, pulled blood samples from herself, labeled them, and stored them in the racks. Examining her work, she gauged her chem set up adequate. Small baggies contained pulverized gemstone samples, the remaining chunks stored in a mesh bag on a string around her neck. Who knew how long the stones would have to last? She'd keep them with her.

"I'm going to need an inventory of what tools we have access to if I'm to get anywhere."

Davis dropped his chair back down on all four legs with a *thump*. "What do you expect me to do about it?"

"Help, or get out of the way," she said.

He pulled out a radio from his jacket pocket and turned it on. The ugly whistle and pop made it clear why it hadn't been on. "Liu wants a tour."

"Proceed," came the response.

Davis stood, pulling his jacket into place and putting the radio and magazine in his pockets. He gestured to the door. "After you."

Cindy glared at him. They'd been through this before. The ridiculously heavy door had proven difficult to manage in her child-sized body. She suspected he made her open it so he could laugh at her struggles. She stalked forward and pushed hard against the door, trying to hide the effort it cost, then gracefully held it open for the much larger man, letting go when he had walked halfway through so the door slammed into his shoulder. When he shot her an accusing look, she gave him her most saccharine smile and skipped down the hallway.

She peered into room after room, finding them mostly unused and in disarray. Such a shame. The facility was large and isolated, two factors that lent a lot of possibilities. Neighbors had often been the bane of Cindy's existence. But understaffed and underfunded led logically to underutilized. What she could have done with this space when she had her full resources at her fingertips! Instead, she'd have to cadge and cobble something together to help arrest her further regression into childhood.

Once, she had worried that age would take her mind, send her wandering the halls of dementia. Now, she worried that she might regress into a concrete operational mode of thinking, losing her hold on abstract ideas and deductive reasoning. It was the meanest sort of irony that her solution led to another problem.

As she scurried through the labs and storage rooms, she made mental notes of various devices and tools that might prove useful. Davis tromped along behind her, not hiding his annoyance very well. Whatever. Not her concern. If she and her father were going to be of use to each other, as he suggested, he'd have to give up on having her followed around by a babysitter. If she made the task onerous enough, maybe it would be sooner. Davis was an asset better allocated elsewhere anyway.

She opened another room, this one lined with machines that looked, as much as anything, like 1950s kitchen appliances. It seemed unlikely the facility would house a bunch of freezers and refrigerators, though, so she looked closer.

They weren't refrigerators.

A graveyard of stabilization machines from the past century spread before her eyes like a museum of outdated technology and failed attempts at stasis. She spotted a sensory deprivation chamber the likes of which she hadn't seen since the 1970s. Mostly, she cared more for biological systems than machines, but years in labs around the world had taught her the tools of her trade. Wavering hope rose in her breast and she moved through the room with more purpose. There might be something she could use. It wouldn't be the same as having her state-of-the-art tools back, but it would be a place to start.

Shoved between a broken MRI table and a specimen storage refrigeration unit missing its door, Cindy found her salvation.

"Help me get this out!" she called to Davis.

He grunted and mumbled something about not being her roadie, but still helped her move the broken equipment out of the way to examine the machine more closely.

Like something out of a Cold War era monster movie, the metal tank had a glassed-in area above where a person's face would go. She recognized it as a precursor to the isolation chamber the mysterious man had destroyed when he took Jessica from her lab. Coupled with some of the resonance imaging hardware, she could make herself a hybrid chamber, something to amplify the effects of her serum and speed up the process.

She jumped up and down squealing, then threw her arms around Davis and hugged him, barely registering his discomfort. "It's perfect!"

12

PATRICIA VS. LEONEL

P atricia arrived at the duck pond in the city park near the hospital a few minutes early, thinking she'd have time to walk and gather her thoughts. It had been years since she'd last been here, but she remembered it fondly from early morning runs when she first moved to Springfield. She bought a bag of approved duck food from the vending machine at the edge of the lake, the city's attempt to discourage people from feeding the birds old bread and other things that made them fat and sick.

At nearly dusk, all the families and children had gone home. Only a jogger or two panted on the paths around the small lake. Lovers tended to gather in the meadow rather than by the water at night, to avoid the mosquitos.

It was a good choice for a quiet and peaceful place to talk. She could see why Leonel had chosen it. She made her way to the water's edge and found Leonel already there, sitting on a large boulder and flinging duck food with a force that made Patricia hope the ducks had the sense to stay back and wait for it to land before gobbling it up. She sat next to him without saying anything. He had called her, after all. She'd wait to see what he had to say.

The bag empty, he crumpled it into a small ball against a rock, which disintegrated under the pressure of his hand. He looked down at the rock dust in surprise and wiped his hands on his pants. Puffy-faced and teary, he'd clearly been crying for a long time. Patricia didn't know what to do with that. She didn't even know what to do when women cried in front of her, and Leonel, at least on the outside, was a man, even if that development was recent. Disturbed, she handed him her bag of duck food and watched as he threw the little nuggets into the water. Some skipped across the surface like rocks. Maybe this wouldn't calm him as much as she hoped.

She cleared her throat, but didn't say anything. A heron waded through the shallows beneath the bridge at the far end of the pond. It stopped, becoming so still it might have been mistaken for statuary before swooping into the water with one fluid motion, then taking to the sky, a fish's tail flapping in its beak.

"I've just come from Jessica's hospital bed." Leonel's voice rumbled, raw and gravely.

"How is she?"

"She'll have another surgery tomorrow or the next day."

Patricia gulped. She didn't know if another surgery was normal under the circumstances, or a last-ditch effort to save Jessica's life. She knew Jessica had been burned badly, of course, but she was no medical professional. Her stomach clenched with guilt, the same guilt that kept her away from the hospital the past two days. Jessica had gotten those burns saving Suzie. She'd never have been injured if Patricia had planned better and taken Helen out efficiently.

"You haven't even been to see her." Despite the flat and emotion-less tone, Patricia felt the sting of the accusation.

"I didn't want to be in the way." She hoped her lame excuse could keep the peace.

Leonel laughed, an ugly and harsh snort that ended in growl. "You mean you didn't want to face what you'd done."

Patricia stood. "Is this why you called me here? To rake me over the coals again for the mess I made? Do you think I don't know?" Her scales rose along with her voice. She didn't need anyone to take her on a guilt trip. She knew how to travel that road all on her own.

126

Leonel stood and leaned in close enough for his spit to mist her face. "Please. You only care about finding Cindy Liu. Not everything is about you and your wounded ego!"

Patricia held her ground. Leonel loomed large, but she couldn't be intimidated by mere size. Plenty of men had tried to make her back down and failed in corporate boardrooms, and she'd taken on champion field hockey players even before she became bulletproof.

"We need to know where she is! She did this to us!" Her scales fully out, the nodules that would grow into spikes formed along her shoulders.

Leonel pushed her.

She hadn't been prepared and wound up backed into a tree, catching a branch in her spikes. The tree bent with a groan as she shook herself loose, then pulled the bark off her spikes and flung it away. She grabbed another branch with a decidedly more claw-like hand and recovered her balance. With a howl of rage, she threw herself at Leonel. He grabbed her wrist and stopped her outstretched talons a couple of inches from his face. When she pulled back, he punched her squarely in the solar plexus. If she weren't so armored, he might have broken bones. Still, she thought she heard something crack.

"This is your fault!" he yelled, throwing another punch that went wild.

Patricia dodged it easily, even with the additional bulk her alter ego added to her frame. She scooted backward, weaving between trees. Leonel followed, breaking off branches and throwing them. Enraged and untrained in any serious kind of fighting, he lumbered like a blinded bear, knocking over a bench and flinging wounded plants from his path as he chased her. A pair of deer fled when a tree fragment landed near where they had been grazing. Their retreat alarmed the birds and the surrounding trees exploded with the squawks of angry and agitated animals.

Patricia took a fighting stance in a flat area about as wide as a boxing ring, the ground covered in low-lying purple and white flowers. Leonel had her on strength, certainly, but she had him on speed and dexterity, as well as training. She'd long been a fan of kickboxing, but hadn't expected needing to use it against a friend.

"I should never have listened to you," he rasped, voice thick with emotion.

Patricia lunged, slicing his bicep as she slid around him and settled back into a ready pose. He clapped a hand over the wound, stunned, and charged her again, telegraphing his punch from several yards away. Patricia dodged and Leonel drove his fist deep into the trunk of a tree, then pulled it out, cut and bleeding from the bark. "I trusted you."

Patricia dropped her hands.

He had trusted her.

They all had.

She braced herself for the hit she knew would come, punishment she deserved for her failure to protect the people who put their faith in her.

Instead, Leonel fell to his knees and howled, loud sobbing tears that shook his entire body. Patricia pulled back her scales and crouched next to him, awkwardly patting his shoulder. She wished he had hit her instead. She knew how to deal with that kind of pain. It came down to endurance and self-reliance. Pain she understood.

Having friends was going to be a lot messier.

THE END

III

THROUGH THICK AND THIN

I

COMING OUT AS LEONEL

INTRODUCTION

When Linda Alvarez took that fateful shower in the first chapter of
Going Through the Change and his journey to become Leonel "Fuerte"
Alvarez began, I knew he could not keep this secret from his family
and friends. His circle was too tight for that. So, this story imagines
the moment when Linda/Leonel has to reveal himself to his best
friend and convince her he is still the same person beneath the skin.
Coming out is always tricky...no matter what you're confessing.

I'm a romantic at heart, and I wanted to write a hero who gets to
keep their circle around them—not without tension, of course. I get
tired of the "heroism is a lonely road" trope that sees family and
friends as liabilities only in a heroic life. So, Leonel, who has always
taken strength from his friends and family, will continue to do so.

COMING OUT AS LEONEL

David Alvarez looked nervous, but Marisol didn't feel sorry for him. Clearly, the man was up to something. It had been weeks since anyone had seen his wife, Linda, and the explanation that made the most sense was that David had done something to her. Marisol no longer believed Linda had fallen ill or that she'd gone on a trip. She hadn't really believed it even then. Linda told her everything. Marisol would have known if her best friend decided to leave town.

When he called this little meeting of Linda's neighborhood friends, Marisol expected him to try to paint himself in the most positive light possible and to make the trouble, whatever it was, sound like Linda's fault. But she never could have guessed this insane angle. He really expected them to believe that this stranger, this *man* that David had brought into their midst was Linda, somehow...transformed?

"You've got to be kidding."

The man who claimed to be Linda Alvarez shook his head. "I know it's hard to believe, Marisol, but it's true." He peered into her face beseechingly, his soft brown eyes full of sadness.

Marisol met the gaze of the other neighborhood women seated on the sofas and chairs, her own doubts mirrored in their faces. Anna's usually soft expression molded into something like concrete, and her arms crossed over her ample chest. She sounded like she'd swallowed something disgusting when she spoke, her voice tightly controlled with the willpower it took to contain her rage. "David, if this is some kind of joke, it's in very poor taste."

David stepped away from the doorway where he'd retreated after introducing this stranger. "It's no joke. *Es mi amor, es Linda.*"

Marisol stood. "That's the craziest thing I've ever heard. You really expect me to believe that this—" she gestured at the man perched at the front of the large green chair across from her, "this *man* is your wife?"

"How can I prove it to you?" the stranger asked, his hands clasped demurely between his knees.

None of the women answered. Anna scowled. Bett stared at her own shoes and chewed a thumbnail. Jean looked as if she might cry.

The man appeared a little teary-eyed himself. "We've been friends for almost twenty years, Marisol," he said. "There has to be a way to make you understand."

Everyone turned to her. Marisol wasn't the oldest woman in the room, but she had always been the leader of their group, the one who arranged block sales and summer pool parties and organized the covered dish sign-up whenever a family needed help. It made sense that the women of the neighborhood would look to her to settle this. But she had no idea what to do. The story David and this man had brought them was beyond preposterous. She couldn't imagine what would motivate David, whom she had always known to be honest and reasonable, to come to them with a story about how his wife had been transformed into a man.

By soap.

Things like that simply didn't happen.

Marisol turned to David. "What really happened, David? Where is Linda?"

Her heart raced as her imagination ran scenario after scenario that could explain this situation. None of the stories ended well for Linda.

Was David delusional? On drugs? Under the influence of some kind of con? Cheating on Linda with a man?

"Where is Linda?" she asked again, louder, fighting to keep the hysteria out of her voice. When they talked about these kinds of things on the news, the friends never suspected a thing. They always described the criminal as an ordinary man, kind to animals and children. No one ever said they got the heebie-jeebies every time he came into the room. Had they been blind to a wolf within their midst?

"I am still Linda," the man said, standing and laying a hand on Marisol's shoulder. She shrugged it off violently, fighting the urge to rub the spot where he touched her. He sighed and ran a hand through his hair, tucked the long strands behind his ears, then tugged on the ends. Marisol gasped, putting a hand to her mouth. It was a familiar gesture, one she knew from long, heartfelt talks with her friend. *It couldn't be.*

Anna bolted from her chair, unable to contain her anger any longer. She staggered toward David, violence crackling from her like summer lightning, palpable and dangerous. "If you've done something to hurt Linda—"

The strange man leaped between Anna and David, a human shield raising his hands in a gesture of surrender. "Anna! You can't think that my husband would hurt me. You know he's never raised a hand against me or our daughters. David is a good man."

Anna didn't look convinced. She closed and opened the fists at her sides. She and the strange man stared into each other's eyes, neither backing down.

David put a hand on the arm of the man protecting him, peering at Marisol over his shoulder. The strange man put his hand over David's and gently squeezed. The tenderness of the touch spoke of physical familiarity between the two men.

Marisol felt sick. She sank into the chair and let her head fall into her hands. After a minute or so of tense silence, she spoke quietly. "Okay. If you're Linda, you should be able to prove it. Tell me something only she would know."

The man smiled. He was gorgeous when he smiled, like a movie star. Antonio Banderas with the muscles of Dwayne Johnson. It didn't make her want to trust him.

With an apologetic nod to Anna, who still scowled at the two men, the stranger crossed the room in two long strides and knelt at Marisol's feet, taking her hands in his. His hands were large, but the nails were carefully manicured and might even have sported a coat of clear polish. "When David and I moved here, you were the first one to welcome us. You brought us a basket filled with cookies you and your daughters had made. They were beautiful, but terrible. David chipped a tooth trying to eat one. I still have the basket. I think of you whenever I use it."

"That's not good enough," Anna interrupted. "David could have told you that. He's trying to make us accept his gigolo by giving him stories to use against us."

David's face turned scarlet with embarrassment. The man who claimed to be Linda stood and returned to Anna. All the women watched, their faces a panorama of dismay. "Anna. When your sister was in the hospital, I picked up your children from school every day. They ate dinner with our family every night for months. When she finally came back home from the hospital, I had to teach you how to make enchiladas the way I do because they had become Shanise's favorite food."

The man turned to the other women in the room, recounting stories and experiences they'd shared, like the time Linda would have gotten a speeding ticket on the way back from the beach if Bett hadn't flirted her way out of it for them. Like the time Jean lost her grocery money in Las Vegas, and the neighborhood took up a collection to keep her husband from finding out. Or the time Rose's husband had gotten drunk and fallen off the back deck then punched David when he tried to help, giving him a huge shiner.

With each story, another set of eyes grew wide. They were all thinking it, but Marisol asked it aloud first. "Linda? Is it really you?"

S ome days later, Marisol agreed to meet Linda for a morning power walk, as they used to do. Once, they might have greeted one another with a hug, but Marisol turned away from her friend's outstretched arm. It was just too weird. It was all so damned weird.

"What should I call you?" In all their recent encounters, Marisol had avoided calling her friend by name, but it was getting awkward. Sometimes you just had to use someone's name.

"I use Leonel as my man name, and it's probably less confusing if you call me that when other people are around, but when it is just us, I would love it if you still called me Linda. Who I am inside has not changed."

Marisol arched an eyebrow and gave her friend a lingering once-over as they stretched. From the stubble stippling his jaw to the prominent biceps and the well-formed thighs discernible through his workout pants, little suggested this was the short, curvy grandmother who had been her best friend all these years. "Well, your outsides sure have changed, Linda." She stopped, turning to look into his eyes, the only place she saw traces of the woman she'd known. "My sister thought I was having an affair when she saw us having lunch."

Linda blushed. "I've been getting a lot of that. When I met my daughter for coffee, people thought I was some kind of dirty old man."

"Old? I don't know how to tell you this, Linda, so I'll just blurt it out like usual. You were pretty when you were a woman, but as a man? Dayum, girl, you got it going on!" Marisol linked her arm with his, but blanched when her breast bumped his arm and let go abruptly.

Linda, sensitive to Marisol's moods as always, reached out to take her hand. "What's the matter?"

Now it was Marisol's turn to blush. "It's so weird, suddenly having this hunk of a man as my friend. I keep thinking you've seen me naked —all those times we took our children swimming and had to share a booth in the locker room."

Linda laughed. Though the voice was deeper, Marisol heard the bouncing cadence of her friend's familiar giggle. Linda dropped her voice to a whisper. "I grew a penis, Marisol. I didn't become a lesbian. David is still *mi vida*. I still like men."

Marisol picked up her pace, stepping ahead so Linda couldn't see the conflict on her face. She tried hard not to imagine the bedroom life of her friends and failed. It was amazing and romantic how Linda and David had been able to stay together and still love each other under the circumstances. It was also beyond bizarre. She couldn't imagine staying married to her own husband should he wake up a woman tomorrow morning.

Thinking of the two of them together made for uncomfortable imaginings, and she fumbled for another topic to distract her. She had so many questions she felt she couldn't ask. Were she and David still intimate? It was a shocking idea, almost as shocking as her best friend becoming a man in the first place.

"You know, when you hid all those weeks, some of us thought you were having plastic surgery."

"*¿De veras?* What did you think I was having done? A face lift? A boob job?" Linda pushed her hands up where her breasts had once been, laughing.

"That was quite the breast reduction!"

The two friends stopped on the corner to catch their breath. A fire truck zoomed around the corner and careened back toward their street. Without a word, they both took off running as fast as they could. Linda, with her new long legs, outstripped Marisol within a block. She paused to wait, but Marisol waved her on when an ambulance rounded the corner, too. "Go! Find out what's happening! I'll catch up!"

By the time Marisol made it back the seven or eight blocks to their street, her lungs burned. She fell heavily onto the bench in front of the still-ugly and fire-damaged old Liu house across the street from Mr. Singh's house and watched, trying to understand what was happening. There didn't seem to be a fire. The truck parked at the end of the block, kitty-corner from Linda and David's, in front of Mr. Singh's house, effectively blocking her view. As the hermit of the neighborhood, the old man was rarely seen out on the street. *Had he had a heart attack or something?*

A boy on a skateboard went by, and Marisol stopped him. It was Bett's son. "Ryan? What's happening down there?"

The boy pointed. "The big tree fell on Mr. Singh's house. The whole thing just pulled up by the roots."

Marisol knew the tree he meant—the huge one the drunk driver hit last summer. That, coupled with the ice storm this winter, must have taken down the ancient oak.

Ryan went on. "They think Mr. Singh is still inside, but they can't budge the tree."

Letting the boy go, Marisol stood and made her way toward the blinking lights. Where was Linda?

A small crowd gathered near Mr. Singh's house. They kept a respectful distance, but also watched the firemen and ambulance crew. Two uniformed men stood beside the tree debating whether to send someone to retrieve a more powerful saw or to use a winch system to remove the tree whole.

Marisol drifted to the side of the group for a better view and gasped at the sight of the house. The giant oak tree that had graced Mr. Singh's yard since before the house was built had simply toppled. Thick roots reached into the sky like the tentacles of a petrified octopus. Lying on its side, the trunk—nearly as wide as Marisol was tall—filled the space between the curb and the house. Branches took up most of the yard, making it impossible to approach the house from the front.

The entire front porch of Mr. Singh's house had caved in, and the upper branches of the tree were embedded in what had once been the living room. She turned to the other neighbors in the crowd. "Does anyone know if he's in there?"

Someone shared that the firemen were breaking in through the back to find out. As they watched, a volunteer fireman ran around the house and reported to the group of emergency workers. Word made it to Marisol's end of the crowd that Mr. Singh was definitely trapped inside but able to talk to the rescue workers. Marisol crossed herself and looked to the sky, thankful the man was, at least, alive. *How were they going to get him out?*

Then, Leonel—Linda—strode across the lawn, the red and white lights of the ambulance flashing behind his—her—head. Without saying anything, he plucked massive limbs off the tree, some as thick as his muscular arms, and tossed them aside as if they were twigs. He broke especially long pieces across his thigh.

The emergency workers and gawking neighbors stopped, stunned into silence. Effortlessly, he snapped off another branch, sending shards of wood flying into the air. He repeated the process, methodically removing the obstacles that kept the rescue workers at bay.

When he finished, Leonel paused, resting his hands on his knees as if winded from a run. By then, the head of the volunteer fire department had recovered from his shock and approached Leonel. Everyone heard him ask, "Who are you?"

"Just a neighbor. You can call me Leonel."

"Thank you for your help, Mister, um, Leonel." He looked around at the crowd, obviously embarrassed and uncomfortable. "I'll need to ask you to get behind the perimeter now and let my men work." The man's face turned scarlet as the onlookers grumbled to each other about gratitude.

Leonel nodded and joined Marisol at the edge of the crowd nearest the house. They both tried to pretend they weren't the crowd's new center of attention.

"That was amazing!" Marisol whispered, reaching over to squeeze Leonel's hand.

Leonel ducked his head, hair falling across his cheeks. He shuffled his feet the same way Linda always had when receiving a compliment. It looked out of place in the body of such a tall and striking man, like a child had taken up residence inside Hercules and needed to go to the bathroom. "I'm glad I could help," he said.

Both friends and the rest of the crowd looked up at the sound of a machine starting. The volunteer firemen had hooked a chain around the denuded trunk and prepared to use a winch attached to the fire truck to pull it away from the house. Eight people in orange vests watched the progress, poised to rush in and retrieve Mr. Singh as soon as they had access to the living room where he lay trapped. Tension silenced the crowd. "I hope *el viejo* is going to be all right," Linda whispered, squeezing Marisol's hand.

Marisol hoped so, too. Mr. Singh might be a bit of a grump, especially with the neighborhood children, but she certainly didn't wish him ill. She wondered if the old man had anyone to care for him. He'd been a widower when he moved into their neighborhood, and she'd never seen him receive visitors. They might have to arrange some meals for him. "Do you think he's very badly hurt?" she asked, gripping Linda's arm, startling at the taut musculature, but not letting go this time.

Linda shook her head. "I hope not. When I was close to the house, I heard him calling out, so he's at least conscious."

The winch whined as it eased the mighty old tree away from the wreckage of the front porch and living room. As the tree shifted, the second story wobbled ominously. Marisol gasped. When they pulled out the tree, nothing would stop the house from collapsing on the lower floor and the old man trapped within. She screamed, along with several other people in the crowd.

The fireman operating the winch couldn't hear them over the noise of the machine and the tree kept moving. Marisol flung her hands over her eyes, unwilling to witness the old man being crushed to death by his own house.

She opened them again when she heard the shocked exclamations of wonder all around her. Dust and debris filled the air, and she tried to wave it away to see what had happened. She cried out in astonishment.

Leonel, no longer by her side, had thrust his body into the hole where the tree had been removed from Mr. Singh's first floor living room and held the sagging second story of the house up with his bare hands. As she watched, Leonel shifted to support the remnants of the outside wall on his shoulders. His newly long arms stretched nearly the length of the wall and his muscles bulged. As he tucked his head to balance the structure across his shoulder, his hair fell across his face, obscuring it.

Marisol burst out of the shocked crowd, ducked under the perimeter tape, and grabbed the astounded paramedic standing beside the gurney in the middle of the yard. "Don't just stand there! Get in there and get Mr. Singh!"

The man shook his head as if clearing it and yelled at his partner to grab the other end. "Let's go!"

As Leonel—impossibly—stood holding up a house, the two men uncovered the old man from the table he had sheltered beneath, got him on the gurney, and removed him from the wreckage. As Mr. Singh passed by on the gurney, everyone heard him say, "I think I hit my head pretty hard. It looks like there's a man holding up my house."

Marisol's eyes welled up with tears. She wasn't sure if she cried from fear, joy, shock, pride, or something else entirely. Whispers and wordless exclamations bounced through the crowd, but she kept her focus on her friend. Around Leonel, the firemen placed metal struts to hold the weight of the upper story. When they said it was safe, Leonel let go of the house, and all of them hurried to a safe distance. The struts creaked and moaned but held.

Leonel sat heavily on the ground, and Marisol ran to his side. "Are you all right?"

"Just tired." Leonel smiled up at his friend. "It's a big house."

Marisol's eyes narrowed. "I don't think you've told me everything yet, Linda."

Leonel flopped on his back. "No," he agreed. "Not quite everything."

II

THE RIGHT THING

INTRODUCTION

This story fits in the Menopausal Superhero universe after the events of book three, so if you haven't read *Face the Change* yet, you risk spoilers if you read this first!

Patricia "The Lizard Woman" O'Neill and mad scientist Cindy Liu's long and complicated friendship continues to be one of my favorite aspects of writing this series. I'm intrigued by long relationships and the shifts in dynamic across them, and this relationship is especially fraught given the nature of their recent history. What happens when you learn your best friend isn't the person you always thought they were?

THE RIGHT THING

Patricia had gone quiet. Never a good sign. Still, her skin remained human—pale and lightly freckled, deeply creased around the eyes and mouth, not a scale in sight. Jessica hoped it meant Patricia would be reasonable. But when Patricia chose to be inscrutable, there was no guessing what went on behind her cold blue eyes.

Now Jessica understood why the Director had sent her to share the bad news. The assignment had nothing to do with her new position as a team leader, or even her history fighting alongside Patricia as Flygirl. No. The Director was just unwilling to face the Lizard Woman of Springfield himself. He'd passed the buck to avoid conflict, and Jessica had fallen for it yet again, just like the time he'd tricked her into telling Leonel about his showy new costume. When would she learn?

"How exactly did this happen?" Patricia's even and modulated voice reminded Jessica of the tone her mother used to hide the boiling rage inside. For a moment, she considered jumping out a window and flying away, passing the buck right back up the chain.

"They're still figuring that out. Like I told you, she was in the lab at ten-thirty, alone, locked in. When the next shift checked in at noon, she had disappeared. There's nothing on the cameras or data logs. No one entered the room. No one left."

"Except Cindy."

Jessica reached out, wanting to offer some kind of comfort. Patricia had known Dr. Cindy Liu all her adult life, longer than Jessica had even been alive. To Jessica, Cindy was a family friend; to Leonel, a neighbor; to Helen, a stranger.

None of them had been happy about the changes Dr. Liu's experiments had wrought in their lives, at least not at the outset. Until she learned to control her flight, Jessica had felt like she'd been handed a disability rather than a gift. But, for Patricia, it had been a betrayal of a completely different nature.

The rest of Liu-vians, as the Unusual Cases Unit (or UCU) nicknamed victims of Cindy's experiments, hardly knew the woman who had ravaged their lives, but Patricia had considered Cindy her closest friend, the one person who understood her and liked her anyway. A forty-something-year friendship etched your soul. It didn't just stop. Not even when your friend does something really terrible, like turning you into a lizard creature with bulletproof scales.

Learning that Cindy had no more compunction about toying with her life than those of complete strangers cast their entire relationship in a singularly unflattering light—one that exposed Patricia as a fool. And Patricia would be no one's fool.

Capturing Cindy Liu had been her quest for nearly two years. When Cindy slipped away in the aftermath of the firefight at the Springfield College campus, Patricia retired to devote herself to finding her once-best-friend and bringing her to justice. She'd succeeded with the help of other agents and had avoided Cindy's case ever since, throwing herself into any mission she could get with gusto of a woman trying to escape herself.

The Department had gained a lot of insight during the months they'd kept Dr. Liu contained and used her own work to mitigate the damage she had done, helping the Liu-vians understand and control the strange changes in their lives.

Patricia claimed to be satisfied with that. She said justice flew loftier than vengeance, even if it didn't quench the fire of her anger, but Jessica wasn't sure she believed her. Working together, Jessica and Leonel had offered support and friendship, giving her space to get past the pain.

But now Cindy had vanished again. The UCU had failed.

The Lizard Woman of Springfield wouldn't take that well.

Patricia stood up, ignoring Jessica's hand, and walked over to the coffee stand. She picked up the carafe, sniffed the contents, then grimaced and put the pot back. She stood with her hands on her hips, seeming to study the wall. Nothing hung there. Not even a bad painting.

"Listen—"

"No." Patricia didn't turn around. Nodules rose and settled underneath her thin blue blouse, threatening a transformation that would shred the delicate material. She gripped the table in front of her, inhaling and exhaling in audible whooshes and huffs.

Finally, Patricia faced Jessica, holding up a hand, the nails only slightly extended. "All you're going to say is you're sorry, and that's stupid. You didn't help her escape. You have nothing to apologize for. And you apologize too much anyway."

"I—" Jessica stopped, realizing she'd been about to apologize for apologizing too much. "You're right. I'm just worried about you." Scales rolled out around her friend's ears and cheeks, then retracted again. Patricia's transformations always disconcerted Jessica, more when the changes seemed to come unbidden.

Patricia sighed. "I'm not the one you should worry about. She's out there again, unsupervised, unchecked. You, of all people, know how dangerous she is." Patricia looked pointedly at Jessica's feet, hovering nearly a foot above the ground.

Jessica burped into her elbow, and her shoes made contact with the floor again. "We'll find her."

Patricia cocked her head at the younger woman, squinting suspiciously. "Who's running point?"

"Sally Ann."

"Well, we've got a shot, then. Where is she?"

"In the green room, I think. Do you want—" But Jessica was already talking to an empty room.

Patricia made a point of looking into every security camera she passed, at least the ones she knew about, and she transformed her face into the most horrifying visage she could muster. She didn't really have a stealth mode, and even if she did, she wouldn't waste time sneaking around now.

No one tried to stop her as she stormed through the halls of the Unusual Crimes Unit to the research wing where Sally Ann Rogers liked to plan an assault.

Sure enough, Patricia found her in the green room, so named because it abutted the botany department. A glass wall profuse with burgeoning plants under pink grow lights cast leafy shadows across the floor and made it easy to forget the institutional setting. Sally Ann said there was more oxygen in that room, which made it a good place to think. It definitely had better light, picking up full spectrum rays necessary for the plants.

Bent over a table examining something through a magnifying device, Sally Ann swiveled her ample hips as if dancing. Even when concentrating, she struggled to be still. She didn't look up when Patricia entered, but waved a hand at a chair at the side of the room. Some kind of elastic tape three shades lighter than her skin bandaged her knuckles. She'd been working out her frustrations in the gym and pushed harder than her flesh could handle again.

Patricia moved a stack of papers onto the floor from the chair indicated and folded herself into the small piece of furniture. Short people always had such ridiculous chairs. The back of this one barely reached the band of Patricia's sports bra, and her knees would hit her chin if she moved too quickly. Patricia took deep, cleansing breaths to calm herself while she waited.

After a few more seconds of examination of whatever she had under the magnifier, Sally Ann stood, stretching her back in a circular motion like some kind of yogi belly dancer. "So you heard, then?"

"Jessica told me. What do you have?" Patricia stood and immediately caught a foot on the pile of papers she'd moved. Several pictures spilled across the floor, and Patricia picked up two. One of Cindy Liu as Patricia had known her three years ago, a sixty-eight-year-old Chinese American woman with a fierce scowl, before she'd experimented on herself. The other showed Cindy as she looked now, a gangly thirteen-year-old child with frighteningly knowledgeable eyes.

"No sightings yet."

Patricia didn't ask about the search. Sally Ann already had their best trackers in the field working their magic. "Any good leads in the lab?"

Sally Ann pressed her lips together and shook her head. "The security footage is clean. And it doesn't show anyone entering or leaving that room."

Patricia picked up a duty roster lying on the table. "Lester was supposed to be in there with her?"

"He got sick. He followed protocol and called it in, but the message didn't go through."

"Why not?"

"Tech is working on that. Some kind of jamming device is my best guess. But that still doesn't explain how she got out of that lab without being seen by surveillance."

Patricia knelt to pick up the rest of the pictures scattered across the floor, slipped them into the folder, and put the stack back in the stupidly short chair. She wasn't good at this part, preferring to leave the puzzling out for cooler heads. She worked best from her gut, leaping first and looking afterward. But now, not knowing which way to leap left Patricia edgy and annoyed. "Can you get me in the lab?"

Sally Ann checked something on her tablet. "They're done in there. Let's go."

P atricia had avoided any contact with Cindy since her former
friend's surrender.

She didn't trust herself.

Once, she would have said she had an instinct for finding good people to surround herself with. Then, Cindy used her as a guinea pig and kidnapped Jessica to forward her precious research. She'd proven she was not the person Patricia believed her to be, but someone far colder, far more manipulative. It called into question every moment of their long friendship. Worse, it made Patricia doubt her own judgment.

Their last night in Paris on their "Forever Young" vacation, Cindy encouraged Patricia to keep their reservation to see the light show on the Eiffel Tower from Place du Trocadero, claiming stomach trouble from the rich food. Cindy said she'd never forgive herself if Patricia missed the chance because of her, so Patricia had gone, feeling guilty for leaving her sick friend alone. Now, she remembered that Cindy had seemed agitated when she returned. Had she really just wanted Patricia out of the way so she could do something Patricia wouldn't approve of?

Patricia found herself rehashing every time Cindy showed up late, arrived disheveled, or canceled at the last minute, examining ordinary moments for clues of a double life and secrets kept. The thought that she'd been a dupe all these years had her gritting her teeth in her sleep, and sometimes her teeth were dangerous.

Once the UCU had Cindy under guard, Patricia had been afraid that if she took any part in Cindy's captivity, Cindy would spot a vulnerability and exploit it, and then whatever havoc followed would be Patricia's fault. So she stayed away. Never even coming to peer at her through the one-way glass. It hadn't mattered. Cindy had found a way, even without Patricia there to use.

Knowing she hadn't been the one to mess up and give Cindy opportunity for escape provided small comfort. In fact, Patricia was confused about why Cindy would even have wanted to escape. The Department had more than fulfilled their side of the bargain and treated her well. They'd provided her with a well-equipped lab and ample resources, including a team of scientists who valued her insights, immediately analyzing her every move and discovery, even if they didn't agree with her methods. It was better than a lot of paying jobs Cindy had worked, and the UCU kept her safe from the enemies she'd made getting this far.

That was more than she deserved after betraying Patricia's trust and manipulating her loyalty. Cindy showed such blatant disregard for what effect her work had on others that Patricia considered letting her enemies have her. There would have been a kind of justice in that. In comparison, working under guard on experimental projects seemed light punishment.

Cindy had never been a social butterfly, so it wasn't like she missed the party scene. She had no family to speak of, and Patricia had been her only friend. Her work had always been her life, and as long as she still had that, she had no reason to run away. Where could she even go?

Standing in front of that well-equipped lab, Patricia looked through the window and waited for Sally Ann to sign off on her access with the guard so they could enter. Patricia had never had a deep interest in science, but she'd learned quite a lot in the months of testing she'd undergone since signing on with the UCU. Genes and mutations. Metabolism. Chromosomes.

Considering the breadth of the changes in all their lives—Jessica, Leonel, even Helen—the microscopic causes were mind-boggling. It was as if her entire Lizard Woman alter ego sprouted from a single freckle on her ankle, something tiny and seemingly unimportant forcing changes that defied logic.

Sally Ann waved off the guard and grabbed the door handle.

Patricia stopped her. "What was she working on?"

Sally Ann shrugged, her face noncommittal. "You know her. Everything."

"But today, specifically."

Sighing, Sally Ann let go of the door and clicked something on her tablet. "Chromatophores."

"Like chameleons?" Patricia had learned a lot about reptiles as the team attempted to explain her own changes to her. Chromatophores had something to do with the transformational aspect of her power, why she could appear human or reptilian at will. Overlapping epidermal scales altered and thickened, making her skin near invulnerable. Her strength and attitude? She came by those naturally.

"Well, yeah. She is an expert on scaly critters, as you might have guessed." She waved a hand at Patricia.

Patricia grimaced. Like she could ever forget. The stupid populace of Springfield had saddled her with the "Lizard Woman" moniker, after all. What started as some kind of eczema had become a full-body transformation thanks to Cindy's manipulations. Lizard Woman was an oversimplification, since Cindy's formula pulled from a variety of reptilian sources, but the nickname stuck. It was kinder than some of the things she had been called in her fifty-seven years.

Considering chameleons, Patricia peered through the glass into the lab. "How was the room searched?"

Sally Ann blinked at her. Nobody could do a cold blank stare like Sally Ann Rogers. Patricia felt a little intimidated, even though she was nearly a foot taller, thirty years older, and fifty pounds heavier than the petite black woman. Not to mention bulletproof.

Patricia cleared her throat. "Any special scans or anything?"

"What do you mean?"

Patricia sighed, closing her eyes. When she opened them again, she had transformed her upper face and eyes. When Patricia had first undergone the transformation to her alter ego, it had taken some time to adjust to "Lizard Vision." The strangeness of viewing the world in terms of heat and movement instead of the kind of detail she saw as a human was so upsetting that she'd had to spend many hours honing her focus and transformation to only affect certain parts of her body.

She saw differently when she wore her lizard face. The extra eyelids afforded protection from smoke and gases. Her night vision sharpened. She also saw a kind of aura around people. Sometimes she could tell when people lied based on the color and intensity of that aura. The medical research team thought it involved a sort of infrared vision, allowing her to see heat. The only heat traces she read in the room at the moment crawled around the tanks at the back of the room.

When she blinked her eyes, appearing human again, Sally Ann stared at her. "That's some freaky shit, right there."

"You're telling me." Patricia opened the door and walked in, letting her gaze bounce all over the room. She didn't know what she was looking for, but she had a feeling there was something to find, something others had overlooked. She stopped and stood at the table where Cindy Liu had last been seen. A cup of tea sat near a notebook filled with chemical formulas written in her backward slanting handwriting.

Remembering that short people leave things down low, Patricia squatted and looked the room over again from the lower position, sliding back and forth between normal and lizard vision. From there, she spotted neatly bundled blue cloth shoved onto a lower shelf under the workstation.

"What was she wearing?"

"A sexy little blue ensemble, somewhere between prison coveralls and hospital scrubs. Why? You thinking of trying a new look?"

Patricia pointed out the bundle. "Looks like maybe Cindy was."

A few minutes later, the lab again swarmed with techs, including one very red-faced young man who confirmed the bundle of clothes had indeed belonged to Dr. Liu, which meant that not only had she escaped their custody, but she had likely done so in the nude. Patricia wondered if the boy would be any less embarrassed if he knew the prisoner was really sixty-eight years old and only looked like a teenager because of dangerous self-experimentation.

When Patricia spotted Walter Peeples among the scientists, she flagged him down. Walter was one of the few members of the science team who spoke "regular person" and just the man she needed to talk to.

"Help me understand what she was working on. Sally Ann said it had something to do with chameleons."

Walter smiled. He and Patricia understood one another. She didn't have to play polite games with him. "She was trying to develop natural camouflage, some kind of cream our agents could apply to blend in with the background. It was still very unstable according to her last report." Walter ran a hand over his head, flattening his short, thinning blond hair against his scalp.

"So, she'd had some success then?"

Cindy wasn't a patient woman. After all, she'd used her fountain of youth formula on herself without other human trials, a risk that nearly cost her own life as she dropped years like used tissues at a Nicholas Sparks flick. She'd tested Patricia's bulletproof flesh by shooting her. Both experiments had the potential for tragedy, but Cindy thought knowledge more important than life itself.

"I hadn't seen anything to make me think she'd had a breakthrough."

Cindy was probably also cagey with her supervising team, not letting them know how far along her research really progressed. Maybe Patricia should have been down here, keeping an eye on things. Everyone had been warned how slippery and manipulative the woman was, but it took first-hand experience to drive the lesson home. Now they'd all learned the hard way.

Walter scanned the lab like there might be a message pinned to one of the walls. His eyes widened. "Now that you mention it..." Walter turned, caught the eye of a young man with bright blue hair and waved him over. "Can you find me the resources list for this lab?" The young man ducked his head and hurried from the room.

Patricia arched an eyebrow at Walter, but he didn't say anything else. He touched her elbow and walked her over to the large rat cage at the back of the lab. Four rats moved around the cages, pacing in circles. Walter seemed especially intent on one particular enclosure: a dark brown rat kept shortening its path. It almost seemed to be avoiding something, though nothing barred its way.

Patricia narrowed her eyes. And transformed them. There was

something there—something she hadn't seen with her human eyes. Something oblong, stretched out across the cage. It seemed to breathe as she watched. "Walter." Patricia reached behind her, but the scientist had moved away. He conferred with the blue-haired man again, their heads bent together over a tablet.

She walked over to them. "Are you, by any chance, missing a rat?"

Both men looked up at her. Walter nodded. "Yes, the disposal report doesn't match the supply report."

"I think I found it."

The lab quickly became crowded as the techs worked to remove a sick rat they could only see when wearing special filtered lenses. Walter called out orders about bloodwork and toxicology as the techs nearly ran into each other in their hurry to exit and obey.

Patricia moved out to the hall and paced. Somewhere in the confusion, Sally Ann disappeared, abandoning Patricia to the science guys. She didn't want to leave in case they learned something, but there was nothing for her to do.

Resting against the wall, she watched the techs rush back and forth, each focused and purposeful. She leaned her head back, and it bounced against the wall with a satisfying thunk like a ripened coconut. Sliding down into a squat, she tried to distract herself from the wait, flexing her arm scaly and smooth in turns and extending her claws to varying lengths.

Even when she'd been Vice President over Marketing in her pre-Lizard days, she'd been a hands-on kind of woman. And right now, she wanted to get her hands on the missing Dr. Liu. If Cindy had done to herself what she'd done to that rat, she could be anywhere.

Even a non-scientist could see that the rat's breathing was labored, well, if they could see the animal itself at least. The techs talked about elevated heart rate and shock before she'd made her exit. None of that sounded good. Infrared goggles replaced her in the lab, so she sat on

SAMANTHA BRYANT

the floor, as useless as a middle schooler at a microscope, able to see the problem but not diagnose it.

Patricia sprang to her feet as the realization struck her. She might well be the only person who could find Cindy!

Patricia transformed in one fluid movement, ignoring the damage to her blouse, and startling the lab techs standing across from her by the lab door. She looked up and down the hall with her enhanced vision, but she didn't see anything she couldn't explain. Cindy wasn't in the hallway. Of course, it had been hours since she disappeared. What did Cindy want and where would she have to go to get it?

She spun on her heel and grabbed the first person who walked by. The man with the blue hair made a small squeaking sound and looked up into Patricia's scaly face with round eyes. Patricia shook her head and pulled her scales back in. "Who found her missing? Who was on shift at noon?"

"I don't know, ma'am."

"Find out!"

The man looked down at the tablet he held and flicked a few things around. "Ernesto Pavel."

Patricia leaned over the young man, trying to look at the screen. He automatically pressed the device to his chest, like a teenaged girl protecting her diary. Patricia suppressed a growl. "Can you find me a picture of Pavel and tell me if he's in the facility right now?" The man narrowed his eyes at her. "Please," she added, practicing the diplomacy the other agents had been trying to teach her. "I've got a hunch, and I need to talk to him."

The man still looked annoyed but complied with her request. He turned the screen around so Patricia could see the ID badge photo of Ernesto Pavel, a thirty-something light-skinned Hispanic man, maybe Brazilian in background, with a substantial mustache almost over-shadowed by truly impressive eyebrows. He had a squarish head and very dark eyes.

Patricia's gaze flicked back to the blue-haired man's face. His mouth had almost disappeared into a tight, straight line, but he met

160

her gaze steadily. "Pavel's on a meal break, so you'll probably find him in the dining hall. Anything else, Ms. O'Neill?"

"Yes." She held out a hand for him to shake. He took it, eyeing her warily as he did. "Thank you. I owe you one, mister...?"

"Jeremy. Jeremy Case."

"Nice to meet you, Jeremy." Patricia saluted the man, then turned to run down the corridor toward the dining hall.

It didn't take long for Patricia to find the man in the sparsely populated hall. She dashed across the room, her ruined blouse streaming around her like a gauzy cape worn over her more durable sports bra, and pulled a chair up to his table, startling Ernesto into dropping his fork on the floor. He pulled his earbuds out and glared at her, unfazed by her sudden appearance. "Can I help you?"

"I really hope so. You reported Cindy Liu missing this afternoon, right?"

He nodded.

"Tell me exactly where you went after you left the lab. Step by step. Don't leave anything out."

"What's this about?"

Patricia rolled her neck, trying to calm herself before she had an unplanned transformation. It wouldn't help her reputation if she unleashed her inner lizard because a colleague annoyed her. She let out a long slow breath, then started again.

"I'm Patricia O'Neill."

"I know who you are. That's not what I asked."

"I was part of the team that brought Cindy Liu in. I've known her for more than forty years. If anyone can find her, it's me. But I need to know exactly what your path was after you found her missing."

Agent Pavel still looked stern, but the softening of his jaw line suggested he might help after all. Patricia endeavored to keep her tone appeasing, something she hadn't practiced much. "Please. She's a danger to herself and others."

"You got that right. Little Liu, she's a piece of work." He whistled.

Patricia held her breath.

Then Pavel started talking.

He guided Patricia through his path. He had arrived for change of shift at noon and found that the previous agent had signed off at ten-thirty, leaving the room locked, but without a guard for ninety minutes. Failing to spot Cindy through the observation glass, he let himself in with his access card and searched the room. When he didn't find her, he contacted security. Per protocol, he stepped into the hall to wait for their arrival to avoid contaminating the scene further.

Once the Department's internal investigative team arrived, he was dispatched to file his formal report. Then, he went to the locker room to change and put in his PT for the day at the gym. The rest of his day was routine, mostly spent processing paperwork. Though he hadn't gone home as planned at suppertime, he had come to the cafeteria to eat.

Patricia stood and offered her hand for the man to shake. Still standing beside his table, she transformed her eyes and scanned the cafeteria carefully. She saw no visible oddities, so she thanked him and returned to the lab. She had a path to follow now.

If Cindy had treated her own flesh with whatever she used on the rats, then she was probably still in the lab when Pavel reported for his shift, just invisible to human vision. When he entered and left the lab, Pavel provided her with the opportunity to slip out unseen. It only made sense that she followed him. She wouldn't know the layout of the building or the location of the exits.

Not bothering with subtlety, Patricia let her scales free as she sped through the corridors, swiveling her head to examine the floors and any obvious hiding places she passed. Human vision wouldn't help her find Cindy anyway. Not if she was right about what her old friend had done. The shape of the rat flashed in her mind, bright red with heat despite the temperature-controlled laboratory—fevered, weak, possibly dying. Cindy would follow suit if Patricia couldn't find her in time.

Retracing Pavel's steps, Patricia burst into the debriefing area and into room four, where Pavel had filed his report. The room was dark and empty, even of invisible inhabitants. Patricia slammed a scaly fist against the doorframe, denting the metal, spun on her heel, and hurried back out, chased by her own sense of urgency and foreboding.

Next, the men's locker room.

Patricia burst into the room to quite a few startled exclamations. Men hastily grabbed items of clothing, but she didn't spare a glance for the masculine nudity on display.

Instead, she dropped to her knees and examined under the benches and along the walls near the towel racks. Another agent emerged from the sauna, clouds of white steam billowing around him. Patricia looked away to give the man time to cover up.

That's when she saw it.

An orange glow in the corner with the towel hampers.

Wordlessly, she rose, pushing past the mostly-nude man still gaping at her as he fumbled to wrap a towel around his waist. She yanked the hampers out and crouched next to the shape. "Cindy?"

No response.

A quick flick of some facial muscles to return to human vision showed her what everyone else in the room must have seen: nothing at all.

But Patricia heard a low moan, soft as a kitten mewing.

Grabbing a towel from the rack, Patricia switched back to her heat-detecting vision and knelt to wrap Cindy's body. She pulled the tiny invisible woman into her arms, grimacing at the clammy feel of Cindy's skin and the labored gasps of her breathing.

"You little idiot," she growled. "How can so someone so smart be so damned stupid?"

Cindy shivered and groaned. Patricia bit down the desire to scream at her. She got to her feet, cradling Cindy against her chest. "Don't just stand there," she yelled at the half-dressed agents staring at her. "Open the damn door."

The man from the sauna scrambled around her, sliding in a puddle on the tile. He pressed himself into the wall as Patricia shoved through, running full speed toward the lab.

Most of the team had dispersed, but blue-haired Jeremy Case was

SAMANTHA BRYANT

still there, standing in the hall tapping his ever-present tablet. "Jeremy! Call medical. Get Walter down here. I found her."

The young man only hesitated a second before he pulled out a phone and dialed.

Patricia lowered her bundle onto an empty lab table, trying to wrap the towel around Cindy's inert body. "What the hell were you thinking?" she hissed, her vision blurred with hot tears. She yanked off her half-shredded shirt and used it to wrap Cindy's legs. Blinking her face human, she flopped into a nearby stool, staring at the towel that held the form of a girl she could no longer see, like something that might have been painted by Dalí.

"You almost killed yourself once already. But you haven't learned a damn thing, have you? You bought yourself another lifetime and still hurtle on like you're running out of time." Patricia groped for Cindy's arm and found her hand mostly by feel. The fingers didn't squeeze her claw back.

Walter burst into the room with two other men close behind, all of them wearing goggles. He pushed Patricia aside and barked orders to the group. A young woman pushing a cart of equipment and monitors followed on their heels.

Patricia stepped back and then stepped back again as the room filled with more people in lab coats. When she backed herself against a cabinet, she worked her way along the wall and out into the hall where she crouched and ran her hands through her spiky red hair, taking deep breaths and trying to calm the whirlwind within her.

A few minutes later, Sally Ann crouched beside her, holding out a cup of coffee. "Here. This is from my secret stash. Not the crap they put in the conference rooms."

Patricia accepted the cup and settled onto her bottom. She breathed in the aromatic scent for a moment before taking a tentative sip. The warmth thawed the tension of her jaw, and she groaned appreciatively. Sally Ann took the cup and handed her a jacket to cover her sports bra. Patricia shrugged into it, deciding she was done trying to wear ordinary blouses from now on.

"So she never actually left." Sally Ann snorted. "Figures."

"Not for lack of trying." Patricia folded her long legs into a cross-legged position to keep from tripping the men and women streaming in and out of the lab and took back the cup of Colombian heaven. "Did you ever figure out where she was trying to go?"

"Not so far. If they can revive her, we can ask."

Patricia snorted that time, ordering herself not to think about the "if" in that sentence. "Like that will do any good. Cindy isn't just a closed book. She's a closed book in a locked box at the bottom of a murky sea."

"You would know."

The two women sipped coffee for a few moments in silence.

Jessica bounded down the hall, taking long leaps to cover the distance faster than any woman her size should be able to do. She was under orders not to fly indoors. Flopping down at Patricia's side, she took her hand. "I just heard. Is she going to be all right?"

"The team is working on her." Patricia turned to the lab behind her, but with the door closed, there was nothing to see or hear. It was up to the lab coats to save Cindy from herself again.

"You did the right thing," Jessica said, squeezing Patricia's fingers. "She'd be dead if you hadn't found her."

Sally Ann laughed then, a loud guffaw that echoed in the empty hall. The other women stared at her while she tried to rein it in. "I'm sorry. It's just...ironic, I guess. If she hadn't changed you into what you are now, there would have been no one to save her. She made her own hero. The universe has a helluva sense of humor, doesn't she?"

Patricia thought of all the times she had wished Cindy dead in the two years since her transformation, all the times she'd considered ending the life of her oldest friend herself. The hunt to bring her in had been as much about vengeance as justice, and if the UCU hadn't been there, she might not have brought Cindy in alive. A desire to squeeze Cindy's skinny little neck boiled up in her, and her hands flexed around her cup automatically.

But, when the moment came, when she realized Cindy might be in danger, she had still tried to help. She hadn't even stopped to think. She just did it. Did that make her pathetic or heroic? Maybe both.

Walter burst out of the room, smacking the door against the wall and jerking a surgical mask from his face. He squatted next to Patricia and laid a hand on her shoulder. "She'll live."

Patricia nodded.

Living was a good place to start.

III

UNDERESTIMATED

INTRODUCTION

Being underestimated is frustrating, but it can also be a kind of super-power. No one expects Suzie, Patricia's former intern who now works as assistant to the Director of the Unusual Cases Unit, to be able to take care of herself in a dangerous situation. She's young, she's little, and she's cute as hell, so most people see her as a triple non-threat. They're wrong, of course.

The way Suzie challenges Patricia's assumptions about other women thrills me. Her character surprised me when she arrived in the story and continues to push boundaries: both mine and Patricia's. She gives me the chance to explore issues of ageism from the younger end of the spectrum and reminds me that we can all learn from each other, regardless of our respective ages or experience levels.

This story fits into the larger world of the series after book three, but it doesn't contain any major spoilers for the rest of the work, so jump right in and find out how amazing Suzie Grayson really is.

UNDERESTIMATED

S uzie Grayson noticed the Indian man in the yellow polo shirt when he came into the café. Spending time with Patricia and the other agents of the Unusual Cases Unit had trained her to pay attention to her surroundings, even when there didn't seem to be any danger, and that included making note of others in the area. She categorized him quickly as one of Springfield's financial district denizens, dressed for a round of golf this beautiful spring afternoon. Good looking enough, in a salesman sort of way—expensive shoes, probably too much cologne. Not dangerous.

Unfortunately, the man noticed her noticing him. They made eye contact, and his face lit up.

Suzie cursed under her breath. This man wasn't her type, but judging by the way his avid gaze roamed over her petite frame, lingering on her collarbone and her crossed ankles under the table, maybe she was his. As she'd feared, he took her glance as an invitation and walked up to her table after procuring his frozen coffee confection. Suzie kept her attention pointedly on her laptop as if she didn't see him, but he cleared his throat to get her attention.

Swallowing a sigh, Suzie met the clueless man's gaze. She didn't disguise her irritation, hoping the man might show a little awareness and back off. Instead, he pulled out the chair noisily and sat down, uninvited. "What are you working on?" He didn't say "sweetheart" out loud, but it oozed out of his smarmy smile.

She held up a finger and clicked a few more items on her document. Then, she closed the laptop and ran her hands across it as if smoothing wrinkles out of the case. The decal of a fish on a bicycle, a gift from Patricia to celebrate six months together, was starting to peel up on one corner, and Suzie stuck it back down firmly without breaking eye contact with the man across from her. She kept her face cold and expressionless, purposely slowing her eye movement so she appeared not to blink.

He began to look uncomfortable, a good sign.

Then, he laid a hand over hers. A bad sign. "Do you want—"

"Is this guy bothering you?" In handling her unwanted tablemate, Suzie had failed to notice when Patricia walked in. Surprising, because it was hard not to notice Patricia O'Neill, even when she wore her human face.

Patricia strode toward the table, ignoring the other patrons watching the drama unfold, arms crossed over her chest and head cocked to one side as she gave the polo-shirt clad man a dismissive up-and-down. In college, Patricia's field hockey team had dubbed her "The Amazon." Now, at nearly sixty years of age, she still towered an unapologetic six-feet tall, strong and confident, and walked with a swagger echoed in the vibrant red of her short-cropped hair.

She loomed behind Suzie's chair, letting the silence stretch uncomfortably long. Suzie couldn't see it, but Patricia was probably doing that thing where she shifted her eyes to their reptilian form just long enough to make a person think he imagined it. She didn't need that trick to intimidate people, but she enjoyed it.

When they first met, back when Suzie had been Patricia's intern, Patricia's hard-nosed attitude and unapologetic forthrightness over-awed Suzie, and that was before she saw her Lizard Woman persona. Even though she knew the woman's softer side now, she was glad Patricia's wrath wasn't directed at her.

"I was just leaving," the man said, pushing the chair back so quickly it squealed against the tile. He hurried out to the street where he stopped and looked at them through the window before scampering toward the big parking garage on the corner.

Suzie sighed. They'd had this conversation several times already. "You didn't have to do that. I had it."

"Of course you did." To her credit, Patricia sounded like she believed it. But she still preened like some kind of rooster and gestured with her thumb at the street. "But it was so much fun to make him squirm."

Suzie decided not to try to make her understand the issue just then. Patricia had come a long way in their time together. She had learned to stop automatically dismissing younger women because they were inexperienced or short or cute or blonde. After all, Suzie was all of those things and a powerhouse of a person, one not afraid to call Patricia on being condescending or smug.

It had gotten more complicated once they started sleeping together. That brought out a protective side of Patricia, which, while flattering, was also annoying and a little patronizing. Suzie didn't need anyone to fight her battles. Certainly not skirmishes like unwanted coffee shop flirtations. You didn't have to be bulletproof to put a pushy man in his place, after all. In a quieter moment at home, she'd try to explain again how moves like that one undercut her own authority and autonomy, suggesting to the world that Suzie was a delicate flower in need of protection.

Suzie stood up, slipped her computer into her bag, and returned her coffee cup to the dish bins. "Come on," she said to Patricia. "If we don't leave now, we'll both be late for the debriefing."

It was a short walk from the coffee shop to headquarters. Patricia nodded to the security guard at the bank that served as the front for the Unusual Cases Unit, then strode across the lobby to the "Employees Only" door near the tellers' stations. She held the door for Suzie who took a bit longer to cover the floor given that she was a foot shorter than Patricia and wearing high heels.

Two security doors later, the pair entered the main hall of the underground offices of the Department. The conference room wasn't well populated yet when they arrived, much to Suzie's relief. She'd still have time to connect her laptop so the Director could use her presentation as he spoke. Suzie liked her support to be so efficient it became almost invisible.

Suzie looked forward to this debriefing. She had played a pivotal role in the agents' success on the Earthquake incident. It had been her first big case after signing with the UCU, and she was proud of her work. Her quick thinking behind the scenes had the getaway car and the distraction ready at the right time. Special agents Flygirl and Fuerte had been able to take the terrorist into custody without inter-ference. There were no serious casualties, and Suzie deserved some of the credit for that, too.

The Director stepped up to the presentation screen, picking up the remote Suzie had thoughtfully placed at his left hand, along with a print copy of his notes. He glanced in her direction and smiled. Suzie smiled back, then frowned when she realized he intended his greeting for the agent behind her.

The debriefing didn't take long. The big takeaway was that the equipment department would upgrade the show uniforms for public-facing agents so they were never unarmed, unshielded, or out of communication, even when trouble was not anticipated. Suzie hadn't gotten the shout-out she expected but tried not to take it to heart. The Director wasn't known for handing out praise. Her work was essen-tial, and she took pride in doing work that mattered in a broad sense. It wasn't always easy to work with people with the unusual powers that UCU agents often manifested, but Suzie wouldn't shy away from a challenge.

Still, a thank you would have been nice.

After the meeting, the other agents, including Patricia, cleared out quickly, leaving Suzie alone to put the room back in order. She gath-ered all the papers and tossed them into the shredding bin, then put the cups and saucers onto a tray by the door so the kitchen staff could reclaim them easily. Coffee from one of the cups splattered her blouse. That was probably going to stain.

Her phone rang. "Suzie speaking."

The Director didn't acknowledge her greeting. "My office, please."

The please was a concession, an improvement in his politeness, so Suzie smiled as she agreed. "Be there in five."

She made it in three, and she'd waited for fifteen by the time the Director arrived. Suzie thought she hid her irritation well. She took down the information about their newest cases, then stood up to leave, intending to return to her own quiet office to organize this mess. The Director stopped her as she neared the door. "Suzie, could you do me a favor?"

"Probably." Giving the man blanket promises wasn't a good idea. He'd smother you with them without ever realizing he'd done so.

"Fuerte wasn't at the meeting. Could you fill him in? Maybe talk to him about the importance of attending debriefings?"

Suzie hesitated. Her to-do list for the afternoon was already quite full of tasks that better fit her job description. Staff management issues should remain on the Director's plate. "That's really not my place."

The Director put on an aw-shucks expression, the one he always used when he didn't want to do something himself. When he pulled that manipulative stuff, even his face seemed to change, making him resemble a young Michael Douglas instead of Michael J. Fox. "He's been so emotional lately. It'll go better coming from you. You have a way with words."

Suzie refrained from rolling her eyes and walked out the door, calling over her shoulder, "I'll let Leonel know you want to talk with him." She wasn't going to let the Director dodge his duties just because emotional displays made him uncomfortable.

Leonel had been through a lot in the past year or so: he'd been transformed into a man, gained super-strength, and gotten shot. To top it off, his husband, who had stuck by his side through all the rest, had walked out when Leonel refused to quit the UCU. Suzie was surprised Leonel held up as well as he did under the circumstances. The Director could suck it up and give his own pep talk.

Back in her office, Suzie spread her notes across the table and began putting the new assignments into her various organizational charts and spreadsheets. As she opened multiple windows on the touch-sensitive screen that made up one entire wall of her office, she appreciated the serious perks of the job, even if it also came with occasional jerks. The tech department was utterly amazing.

Suzie was deeply involved in converting the Director's vague notes into workable plans with appropriate resource allocation and budget codes applied, when someone in the doorway cleared her throat. "It's six o'clock," Patricia said, leaning against the doorframe and letting her gaze bounce around Suzie's open windows. Suzie minimized them all by tapping a pattern on her desk, cuing the system to close the virtual display. She didn't like people seeing her unfinished work, especially not Patricia. Letting the audience peek behind the curtain spoiled the magic.

"I'll be a while yet." Suzie reached around her former boss and closed the door to afford them a little privacy, or at least the illusion of privacy. The entire facility was very well surveilled, but they hadn't told anyone else about the shift in their relationship. Suzie wanted to protect that secret as long as she could. "Do you want to wait? Or meet up later?"

Patricia frowned. After all her years as the VP of a multi-million-dollar company before joining the UCU, she hadn't adjusted to the idea that not everyone was at her beck and call. Suzie watched her convince herself not to push back. "I guess I could put in gym time. Think another hour is enough?"

She could have used two, but Suzie recognized a peace offering when she saw one. "That sounds great. Maybe we can hit the new Thai place for dinner."

Patricia leaned down and kissed Suzie then, bending her back against the desk with a pressure that left her breathless. "Don't make me wait too long," she said. Then the older woman stepped back, smoothed her clothes and the nodules of spikes that had risen on her neck, and walked back out.

Suzie shook her head to clear the endorphin fuzz from her brain and turned back to her tasks, tapping the pattern on her desk to bring all her windows back. It took a few more shakes of her head before she could focus again. If spikes rose up out of her skin like Patricia, she'd have shredded her coffee-stained blouse.

Time sped by as she worked, and when she looked up again, it was nearly seven. Sighing, she closed the not-quite finished plans and promised herself she'd come in early tomorrow to get them done. Right on cue, Patricia rapped on the doorframe. "Ready?" Suzie picked up her purse and keys and followed Patricia to the parking garage.

They had the usual tussle over who would drive. This time Patricia acquiesced and folded herself into Suzie's tiny blue sports car, adjusting the seat as far back as it would go.

They arrived at the restaurant at seven-thirty and were immediately seated. They must have lucked into a lull between crowds. By the time the food arrived, the place was packed to the rafters and so noisy it made Suzie's teeth ache. After dinner, it was a relief to get back out into the comparatively quiet night. "Let's walk for a little while," she said, slipping her elbow into Patricia's. "There's a great moon tonight."

The moon shone large and heavy in the autumn sky. A light breeze fluttered the drying leaves and released a pleasantly musky scent into the air. One of the advantages of spending time with Patricia O'Neill was walking through the city park at night and knowing there's nothing in it scarier than your girlfriend. Suzie didn't even turn when she heard footsteps approaching from behind. Instead, she stood on her tiptoes and pulled Patricia's face down to hers for a kiss.

"Well, isn't that a sight? I know things are pretty liberal in Springfield these days, but I didn't know bestiality was off the books."

Patricia already half transformed before she'd fully broken off the kiss and turned to face their heckler.

Suzie reached out and touched the tree behind her for balance. She pushed her hair out of her eyes to see who was about to get pounded.

She froze.

The man from the coffee shop.

He wasn't wearing a polo shirt anymore, having traded it for something slick and a bit shiny, what Leonel called a gigolo shirt, but it was definitely the same man.

Suzie reached for Patricia's arm too late. The Lizard Woman was already in action, grabbing the man by the stiff collar of his shirt, twisting it to force him into a backbend. Suzie had time to register the man's inappropriate grin before someone grabbed her from behind. She tried to twist out of the second man's grasp, but he had already restrained her hands with something, maybe a zip tie, and pressed a gun into her throat. "Let him go," he said.

Patricia snapped her now completely scale-covered head in the gunman's direction, her yellow eyes narrowing with anger. The spikes protruding from her upper back rose more fully. She was a terrifying sight, even for Suzie.

The man Patricia had been holding fell to the sidewalk in an ungraceful heap when she dropped him. He got up, dusted off his knees, and laughed. "Wow. I mean that was amazing. It's one thing to see you on video, but in person? They're going to come out of the woodwork to see this."

Patricia flexed, and the scales along her right arm rippled. She didn't say anything. It was scarier when she didn't.

Suzie kept still, waiting to see what would happen. Anger crackled off Patricia like lightning, and she prayed it wouldn't make her do anything stupid. Suzie wasn't the bulletproof one. She expected her captor to turn his gun on the Lizard Woman like most criminals, but he didn't. Instead, he kept it against Suzie's neck, increasing the pressure when Patricia stepped toward him, as if he planned to stab Suzie with the barrel instead of shooting her.

Her captor tugged Suzie backward, and she went limp, trying to turn herself into dead weight. It didn't do much good. She weighed all of a hundred and ten pounds. He pulled her up onto his hip and simply carried her, shoving the gun into her ribcage. He made sure Patricia could see what he was doing before he walked away.

"Come on then," said the Indian man in the shiny shirt, following them. "You've got another date tonight." He stopped and picked up Suzie's purse, wrapping the long strap around his wrist. She tried to memorize his face, planning to make sure this man got what was coming to him. She hadn't gotten a good look at the man carrying her so unceremoniously yet, but she'd already spotted the tattoo on his left hand in the shape of a fiery sun, flames spreading onto his thumb and fingers. The UCU could ID him from that alone.

They must have made an odd sight, the large man carrying the small blond woman while the Lizard Woman of Springfield and an Indian man with his shiny shirt open nearly to the waist—the buttons failed to survive his encounter with Patricia—followed a few steps behind. Suzie didn't struggle. She couldn't effect much damage in this position, so she conserved her energy for a single hit when she had an opportunity to make good use of it.

The men probably thought she had already given up, and that was fine. It wasn't always a bad thing to have people underestimate you, especially your enemies. She swiveled her head around, looking for someone to make eye contact with, someone who might call for help. But the men had chosen their moment well. This part of the park was completely deserted. Suzie cursed herself for her lack of caution. The idea of being used to force cooperation from Patricia had her boiling with rage. Fear of this kind of manipulation was the reason so many UCU agents lived alone.

Suzie pushed down her rage and turned back to analyzing the situation. These men had recognized Patricia in her human form, which showed they'd done some research. Not that Patricia had been especially careful. She wasn't big on the protect-your-secret-identity thing, trusting instead in her ability to defend herself should the need arise. "I'm too old to pretend I'm someone I'm not," she always said. There was truth in that, but Patricia took pride in her strength. While she said she didn't want to live in the public eye, part of her definitely wanted the world to know who exactly they battled when she put them in their places. Those wide and scaly shoulders carried more than one chip.

Plastic dug into Suzie's wrists as they pressed against the man's hard chest. He wore Kevlar or something like it under his shirt. If not, then he was something more than human himself. She wanted to shift her position, to take some pressure off, but didn't want to squirm in her captor's arms like some kind of fish. She also didn't know how sensitive his weapon might be. She'd learned a bit about firearms—

even the office staff had basic weapons training at the UCU—but she hadn't gotten a look at the gun yet.

Then he shoved her into the passenger seat of a van and jerked a bag over her head. It smelled of perfume, and the sweet scent nearly gagged her.

Though muffled through the bag, the other voices were clear enough.

"Get in the back," a deep voice ordered.

"What, can't even offer a lady a proper seat?"

Suzie wanted to laugh, hearing Patricia describe herself as a lady.

The Indian man sounded exasperated. "Get in the back like a good girl, or we'll put a few extra holes in your girlfriend."

The big man, who apparently still stood next to Suzie, laughed harshly. Patricia growled, but must have complied. Metal doors slid closed, and then the vehicle lurched into motion.

Suzie tried to track their turns and distances, but quickly realized that without a visual reference, it was a futile exercise. She wondered where her purse was, and if her cell phone was still in it. She had a specially designed back-up model that looked like a hairbrush, another marvelous toy from the tech department. Even if they'd tossed her smartphone, they'd probably missed that. So, if they hadn't tossed her purse entirely, she ought to be able to use it.

The men didn't talk as the van maneuvered through traffic. Patricia was silent in the back, and Suzie worried about what they'd done to restrain her. In her lizard form, Patricia's tough flesh deflected bullets but didn't make her completely invulnerable. Not that it would stop her from taking terrible risks. If their assailants had restrained Patricia properly, at least she wouldn't hurl herself from a moving vehicle or something equally crazy.

After twenty or maybe thirty minutes, the van's tires rumbled over gravel instead of pavement. They'd either gone to the industrial parks bordering Springfield on the north, or to some private estate on the east. Suzie couldn't think of a single place with a long stretch of gravel road within thirty minutes of downtown in the other directions. She'd studied maps and satellite pictures as well as explored the city in person over the past few months. The UCU had excellent mapping software, but sometimes it paid to know things that didn't show up on maps, like abandoned subway tunnels and half-constructed bridges. You never knew what information might prove useful.

When the van stopped, one of the men tugged her out of the vehicle and tried to pull her along. Suzie stumbled exaggeratedly on the gravel. It wasn't a hard sell, especially given her high heeled shoes and, as she hoped, her frustrated captor yanked the bag off her head. "Better?" he asked.

Suzie nodded, memorizing the man's face. He was a meaty sort of man, broad in shoulder and brow alike. White, around forty to forty-five years old, with a nice jagged scar across his left cheek that should make him even easier for the UCU to identify. All she had to do was get word to them. The brute had her purse in the crook of his arm, and Suzie fought to keep a straight face when she saw it. If she could get a moment unobserved within a few yards of her purse, she could activate the Bluetooth headset that had gone unnoticed beneath her cloud of blond curls. She had programmed a few emergency voice commands that could dispatch a rescue team.

The Indian man and Patricia didn't follow.

Suzie walked ahead of her captor, who pressed his gun into her lower back and shadowed her steps in a way that kept his body close to hers. Not wanting to invite more physical contact than necessary, Suzie maintained as quick a pace as she could manage while still trying to make note of their surroundings. They must have gone north because they were in a wide parking lot ringed with large, warehouse-style buildings. She couldn't see any company logos and guessed the buildings were either unoccupied or unlabeled on the back side.

On the other hand, the big beige monstrosity he directed her toward had a giant vinyl banner stretched across the outside wall, advertising a cage match between The Lizard Woman of Springfield and The Crocodile. The pixelated image of Patricia had obviously been pulled from one of the cell phone videos circulating on YouTube. "The Crocodile" wasn't pictured.

Now the comment about people "coming out of the woodwork" made sense. They planned to put Patricia on display and use Suzie to make her fight someone. Suzie didn't know what made her angrier: the plan itself, or the way they used her to make it work. These guys would pay. She'd see to that, one way or another.

When they got to the door, the gunman pulled Suzie against his side and knocked on the door with the gun. He stepped back, tugging Suzie along with him. After a moment or two, the door swung open and a young man peeked around the corner. He had long muscled arms, a lean, wiry frame, and long, dark hair that covered most of his face. "Where's Rohit?" The man spoke as if he had his mouth full.

"Supervising," the armed man holding Suzie said, gesturing back toward the van.

The young newcomer flipped his hair back, and Suzie suppressed a gasp at the sight of the man's disfigured face. His cheeks were bumpy and scaly, but a pale brown flesh color rather than green like Patricia's scales. His teeth protruded from the top and bottom of his elongated, snout-like mouth like stalactites and stalagmites. He had large, soulful brown eyes with a bit of gold in them, bedroom eyes that might have made him quite a Lothario in a less terrifying face. This had to be The Crocodile, Patricia's opponent.

To all appearances, he was just a human with a skin condition and minor malformation of the jaw. Were they really going to put this boy up against Patricia?

He and Suzie sized each other up for a moment, and then the young man turned and stalked off. Suzie watched him, considering what use she might make of the fear and hesitation she'd read in those lovely, liquid-brown eyes. "Come on," he called back. "Let's get her in the box. We need to make sure the Lizard can see her."

The room they took her to was mostly bare with a large glass window facing the floor below. The big guy shoved Suzie, and she stumbled against the glass awkwardly, trying to use the momentum of the fall to activate the button on her Bluetooth headset, but the angle was wrong and she just ended up bruising her cheek. She didn't get much of a look before the brute pulled her away from the window, but she did see a large cage of thick metal bars under some lights at the center of a vast and empty room, like something the circus might use to house the big cat act.

The man tossed her purse into a corner, then shoved her into a chair and slipped some kind of strap across her chest and another across her ankles. As she'd been taught in her orientation training, Suzie pushed her body out as wide as she could and held it flexed while the man affixed her straps. Even an inch or two of wiggle room could make a difference when she got an opportunity to use it. She wasn't sure it had done any good. The straps felt pretty darn tight.

"You got this? I should go help Ro."

The Crocodile nodded and fiddled with some video equipment in the corner of the room. A bright light came on and Suzie's image appeared on a television screen at the top of the window, a feed she was sure would be visible to Patricia as well. She hoped her cheek wasn't swelling from her encounter with the window. If Patricia thought she'd been beaten, her rage might make her foolhardy.

"So, you're The Crocodile?" she said.

The boy grimaced but didn't answer. He continued to fiddle with the camera.

She let a little laugh encroach on her words. "Are you really going to fight the Lizard Woman?"

He stepped over to the window, turning his back to her. He gave a decent show of ignoring her, but she saw the stiffness in his shoulders. Her first guess was right—his ego was easily bruised.

She widened her eyes in exaggerated surprise. "Aren't you worried about her claws? You've seen the videos, right?"

"Let me worry about that. You should be worried about what's going to happen to you." It sounded like a line he'd been fed and didn't quite believe. Suzie detected false bravado and doubt—maybe about the plan, maybe about his role in it.

He puffed out his chest, which only made him seem younger. "She's just a woman. And Ro's a genius. The armor he designed will protect me," the boy went on, a note of little brother pride unmistakable in the brag. Next he'd tell her his dad could beat up hers.

Suzie laced her voice with sympathy. "But you're the one who will be in there with her."

The boy moved quickly for the first time, his hands balling into fists. Suzie braced, fully expecting that she had pushed him too far and that he was going to strike her. She tried to remember what the dental coverage she'd signed up for had included. But the door opened, and his hand fell. Suzie turned her head as far as she could and caught a sideways glimpse of shiny-shirt man, Rohit. "She's in the cage. We all set here?"

The boy nodded. "The camera will feed live to the screen in the cage."

Rohit smiled. He pulled the younger man into an embrace, then pushed him back. Resting one hand on each of the other man's shoulders, he looked into his face. "We've got this, brother. The armor will keep you safe. One night, one fight, and we'll have all the money we need. You've got this."

The boy ducked his head, seeming to agree. His hair covered his face again, so Suzie had no idea what expression it bore. She could see the tension in his body as he took his leave.

When they were alone, Rohit rolled his neck, popping it noisily. He walked up to the glass. With his hands in his pockets, he rocked back and forth on his heels.

Suzie put a whine into her voice. "What are you going to do to me?" It wasn't a bad performance, even if she hadn't been able to muster tears to go with it.

"Don't worry, Blondie. So long as your girlfriend does her part, nothing too bad will happen to you."

Suzie looked into the camera, wondering if Patricia watched this conversation. She winked the eye Rohit couldn't see, trying to signal that she was fine. She forced a shake into her voice, trying to sound young and afraid without making herself laugh. "What have you done with her?"

"She's in her place, waiting." Rohit sounded smug, and Suzie renewed her vow to see him punished for his impudence.

"Can I see her?" Suzie didn't have to fake the catch in her voice, though she was worried for different reasons than this scumbag assumed.

"Sure, sweetheart. Let's give a little motivational pep talk. After all, the crowd should get what it's paying for." Rohit clicked the remote he held, and the image on the screen split. The left half showed Patricia standing in the center of the lion's cage, her body only partially armored. Patricia must be conserving her energy, too. The right half showed Suzie's pale face, washed out under the extra bright light, one cheek purpled. *Damn. It's already swollen.*

Suzie could have sworn Patricia's eyes flashed red, but it was probably just the glare from the camera lens. "I'm all right," she said, her voice absolutely level and clear.

Patricia growled and stepped forward.

"Now, now, love, I wouldn't do that," said Rohit, bending down behind Suzie to put his face next to hers, his cheek stubble scraping her ear. "Those bars are electrified, remember? You found that out the hard way once."

Patricia stopped, cradling a visibly charred forearm. She glared straight into the camera, raising her spikes menacingly. "If you lay a hand on her…"

Rohit ran a hand down Suzie's cheek. "There's no reason to mess up such a pretty face. Not so long as you do as you're told."

Suzie resisted the urge to bash her head against Rohit's face. It would have made her feel better, but it wouldn't help the overall situation. Not yet. She pulled away from Rohit's grasp and he stood and clicked off the television.

Suzie tugged at the plastic bands binding her wrists. A rough edge stuck out, and Suzie pressed so it would slide across the bony part of the wrist. She wriggled it until she felt a warm, moist trickle of blood. She moaned softly. "Please, my wrists. They hurt so much." Suzie looked up at him through her hair, opening her eyes wide to appear frightened and vulnerable.

It worked. His face softened. He knelt behind her chair and *tsked* when he saw the blood. Suzie heard the slow spring noise of a pocket knife opening and then her wrists were free. She twisted to bring them into her lap, leaving a smear of blood across her skirt, and rubbed them. She hoped the man would leave her hands unbound, but apparently he was more wily, or cautious, than that. He pulled a hand-kerchief from his pocket and folded it into a triangle, then used it to bind her wrists together. It wasn't as good as she'd hoped for, but the change still afforded her quite a bit of freedom to move, at least for her lower arms, and that opened up possibilities. Her hands were in front now, too. "Thank you," she said breathily.

A radio crackled. "Ro?"

He picked it up. "Yes?"

"You set? Should I open the doors? The crowd is getting antsy out here."

Rohit shot an assessing look at Suzie. She slumped in her seat, wishing she could muster some tears to sell her weakness more thoroughly, but she was too angry to cry.

He clicked the radio again. "I'd better make sure Sai is ready. Five minutes." He walked to the door, pulled it open, then called back over his shoulder, "You just stay put, sweetheart. It'll all be over soon." Some rattling indicated the locking of the door, and then he left.

Suzie didn't waste any time. She stretched her arm up as high as her restraints allowed and bowed her head painfully until, with a knuckle, she could push the button on the Bluetooth headset still clipped around her ear. "S.O.S," she said, gratified by a whooshing sound coming from her purse in the corner of the room. The preset command sent a text message to the team on call and enabled the GPS signal in her phone. Now, no matter what happened, help was on the way.

Not that she planned to stay put and wait. There was no way they would put Patricia on display like some kind of animal. No matter what Rohit claimed, the so-called crocodile was just a man. Still a boy, really. Suzie wouldn't be surprised if his age still ended in "teen." Even before she'd grown scales and armor, Patricia would have made mincemeat of him, high-tech armor or not. Now, with Suzie threatened to motivate Patricia, he didn't stand a chance.

In case Patricia could still see her, she turned to the camera, winked, and blew a kiss. It was the best she could do to signal she was okay. In the arena below, someone turned on shifting, colorful lights and loud music throbbing with bass. Someone shouted into the microphone, eliciting a squeal that made her wince. Good. The preparations would be loud. That would help.

Suzie rocked the chair back and forth. She'd done this once in a training session, but she was pretty sure they had taken it easy on her. People tended to do that, and Suzie was guilty of letting them when it meant she could avoid pain or hard physical labor. She didn't remember it being so difficult to get the chair to fall. When she finally succeeded, she wished she hadn't. Her head bounced against the wooden back of the chair, and she saw stars. She lay there for what felt like ten minutes but was probably more like two. She tasted blood. She must have bitten her tongue.

Then, Suzie shimmied her upper body like she'd been taught, hoping her flexing trick at the outset had given her a little wiggle room. It had. As she undulated her upper body in rotations a belly dancer would have been proud of, the strap across her upper arms slid upward. With a few more jerks of her torso, the strap slid around her neck, then over her head. Suzie wanted to hoot in triumph, but quickly realized that freeing her upper body didn't get her back use of her hands or feet.

There was a multi-tool in her purse, hidden inside a lipstick case. She'd laughed when Miguel from tech presented it to her, asking him if his name shouldn't be "Q." It didn't seem silly now. It seemed ingenious.

Suzie began the laborious process of dragging a chair attached to her feet across the small room. She managed it by crawling on her forearms and knees, the chair resting awkwardly against her backside and slapping against her with each forward tug. Suzie hoped the camera couldn't see this part. Patricia would tease her mercilessly about escaping by spanking herself repeatedly with a chair. At least she hoped Patricia would get the chance.

Her escape was making a lot of noise. Suzie hoped it wasn't more noise than the music and crowd below. This seemed like a three-man

SAMANTHA BRYANT

operation and, if that was the case, she had a chance. If Sai was preparing to fight, the meat-faced man served as the doorman and bouncer, and Rohit ran the show as impresario and idea man; that didn't leave anyone to notice odd thuds coming from the room where they'd locked the poor, helpless hostage.

With another clatter, Suzie managed to pull her purse on herself, spilling the contents—including her multi-tool. Getting the damned thing open was awkward with her handkerchief-bound hands, but once she managed it, she cut the leg strap and rubbed her tingling ankles with a blood-smeared hand, trying to get the feeling back before she stood.

She wobbled a little unsteadily though she'd taken off her shoes, but she made her way to the observation glass at the front of the box, pausing to turn off the camera in case someone used it to monitor her. This room must have been meant for observing the floor below. Suzie could easily imagine a ruthless overseer keeping tabs on the underpaid workers below. It definitely had a commanding view of the facility.

The large, wide-open room had probably been a sweatshop in its heyday, but now it was empty except for the cage and the crowd of people milling about. The oblong structure squatted right in the middle of the room, a spotlight shining on it. The cage was attached to an external generator, a small secondary fence forming a circular perimeter around it. Suzie could only see one shape moving around inside but knew Patricia was the beast pacing.

A few people wandered around the blocked off area, taking pictures. Other people streamed in through a door in the middle of the far wall. A t-shirt vendor and a few snack stands lined one wall. The room filled as Suzie watched, and the noise became deafening. Arena rock blared through a makeshift and badly balanced sound system. The vibrations shook the walls and floor of Suzie's sky-box prison. The bass rattled the equipment around her. Even the door shook in its frame.

Tearing her eyes from the spectacle below, Suzie made a quick assessment of the room. It would have been too much to hope that anything up here would allow her to influence the equipment down there. The only thing in the room that even had power was the camera, still pointed where her chair had been.

By her count, it had been about fifteen minutes since she'd sent her S.O.S. If the team had responded instantly, it would still be another fifteen before they'd arrive. And there was no guarantee they'd been able to assemble and dispatch quickly. A lot could happen in that amount of time. Patricia could do serious damage to the foolish Crocodile boy who trusted body armor to protect him.

"Not on my watch," Suzie whispered to herself.

Picking up her high heels, she slid her Michael Kors purse strap across her shoulder, and strode to the door. She pressed her ear against it but couldn't determine if anyone waited on the other side over the din of the arena rock and gathering spectators below. Taking a deep breath, she tried the door handle and found it locked, as she'd expected.

Kneeling, she shined the light from her multi-tool on the lock. It was a simple mechanism, probably original to the building. She set to work with the lock-picking tools.

It took longer than she would have liked, and she was sweating and frustrated by the time the mechanism finally turned. When she got back to work, she was signing up for lock-pick training again. Obviously, she needed a great deal more practice.

After a slow, steadying breath, she flung the door open, then pressed herself against the wall, readying herself should anyone investigate the noise. She paused for a count of one...two...three.

Nothing happened, so she knelt on the floor and peeked out, hoping the unexpected height of her head would keep it from getting it shot off by Meat-face or anyone else who might be standing guard.

The hall was empty. Suzie crept to the head of the stairs as soundlessly as she could manage. Peering down the stairwell, she could make out a man standing at the foot of the stairs. She couldn't be sure, but it looked like Meat-face. He was the right shape and size at least, too big for her to take down without a weapon. Suppressing a curse, she backtracked to the sky box doorway.

The entire crowd seemed to cry out at once. The fight must have started. She looked around, seeking options. A little farther down the hall, she thought she saw another door and padded her way down there to explore. Sure enough, it was a door, but the warning sign on it made Suzie's heart sink. "Catwalk access. Authorized Personnel Only."

Suzie glanced over her shoulder as if help might suddenly appear, but she saw no better option. For all she knew, help wasn't even on the way yet. Waiting might mean bloodshed and consequences no one wanted to face.

Steeling herself, she tightened the strap to keep her bag from bouncing against anything and opened the door. The noise from the floor below pelted her like a snowball to the face, and she gripped the catwalk railing with her free hand. Luckily, the bottom of the narrow walkway was solid, rather than metal grating like the one in her high school auditorium. That made it a little easier to talk herself into walking out further.

Each step made the structure rattle. Suzie tried not to think about how old the catwalks were or how much rust might have damaged the bolts and fixtures. She slid one foot out in front of the other and scooted steadily toward the center of the warehouse.

Once she got out a few more feet, she found the courage to look around. Walkways covered the ceiling from one side of the open floor to the other, where a second sky box sat dark and empty. She ignored the dizzy feeling the height elicited. Each time the crowd roared or the music peaked, her perch shook and rattled perilously and Suzie fought the urge to curl up in a ball. She kept moving forward until she was right above the cage itself.

The thud of collisions echoed over the yelling and catcalling of the lookers-on. She stretched out flat on her stomach and pushed her head beyond the protective railings to look below. Fully armored, Patricia's spikes extended to maximum lengths and impenetrable scales covered her flesh, glinting under the harsh light. Elongated and tipped with vicious nails, her dragon feet spread in a fighting stance. She thrust her taloned hands out as she roared.

She was magnificent.

And pissed.

A man dressed almost entirely in red armor stood opposite her. Only his face was visible, but it was The Crocodile, all right. The cracked helmet exposed one side of his distended and malformed jaw, and Sai's cheek bled along a jagged cut. He must have gotten too close.

Pulling her attention away from the fight, Suzie stretched further, trying to get a better look at the equipment off to the side. Rohit sat behind a control panel attached to a generator, watching the fight with rapt attention. His leg bounced up and down, and he gripped the arm rests with knuckle-whitening intensity. His mouth moved, but Suzie couldn't make out what he called out over the crowd noise.

Suzie smiled. None of them were giving her a thought.

She examined the equipment. The ancient and patched-together generator's protective casing was entirely missing, exposing all of its moving parts. Suzie pulled her head back, got up onto her hands and knees, and crawled a few feet farther down the catwalk, her bag bouncing against her belly and thighs. She wished she'd thought of crawling earlier. It was easier to make herself move when she couldn't see how high up she was.

Sitting cross-legged with her open purse in her lap, Suzie dug through it, looking for projectiles. She found a small sewing kit in a solid metal box. It had been a gift from her father. "You never know how it might be useful," he said. *You never know, indeed,* Suzie thought. *Thanks, Dad.*

She held the chunk of metal in her hand. Although only the size of a box of cards, it was weighty. It might do the job, but she'd only get one shot. She didn't know what else she could throw if it failed.

She stood and leaned out as far over the railing as she dared, raised her right hand, and channeled her inner softball player. Aiming for the rotating parts at the center of the device, she pulled back and threw the sewing kit with all her might.

The effect was instantaneous.

For a second, the lights went out. But it only lasted a heartbeat. With a loud grinding sound, it all flickered back to life. The crowd booed and hissed, and Rohit turned and waved at someone behind him, yelling something Suzie couldn't hear. She jerked back, but he didn't look up. Apparently, he thought the outage a malfunction of the machine, not active sabotage.

That meant she could try again, if she could find anything else to throw.

She dug through her purse frantically, but found nothing more dangerous than a breath mint, unless she wanted to chuck her phone or the fabulous multi-tool. And she really didn't. She knew how much it cost to create them.

Then, beside the purse, she spotted her shoes. She had carried them with her, hoping to need them again outside. They were sturdy, with solid three-inch heels. Definitely not as easy to throw, but Suzie had a good arm. And Patricia needed her.

She picked up a shoe and shifted it in her hand, trying a few different positions before gripping it by the toe to execute a strong overhand flick. Suzie aimed and flung her shoe into the center of the generator.

Bullseye!

With sparks and a terrible grinding sound, the spotlight went out, leaving only the fluorescent lighting in the warehouse space.

The crowd didn't hesitate to panic. They shoved and pulled at each other, some scrambling for the exit while others tried to keep their places on the floor. Fights broke out all over. Screaming and shouting filled the air. Rohit ducked and cowered on the floor, making no attempt to quell the chaos.

A clang of metal against metal sounded, and Suzie scooted around to see Patricia pinning Sai against the bars, one scaly elbow thrust into his throat, the other beckoning for Rohit squatting behind his inert control panel, frozen into inaction. After a moment, Rohit raised his arms in a gesture of surrender and stood, scanning the room, probably looking for Meat-face.

Patricia bellowed. Suzie couldn't make out the words but understood the menace clearly.

So did Rohit, because a moment later he scurried over and opened the cage with trembling hands. He threw the door open and stumbled back.

Patricia hefted The Crocodile, still clad in his brilliant red armor, and threw him out of the cage where he collided with his brother. Both men fell to the floor, now mostly deserted of spectators. Patricia walked over and rested a heavy, taloned foot on the pair of them, and flexed, making both men grimace with pain. Flashes from cell phone cameras in the hands of the few fight fans who hadn't fled popped like fireflies in the dim. "Suzie!" she bellowed.

Suzie yelled back, but her words were swallowed by the crowd murmur. Patricia shouted again, pushing harder on the men under her foot. Rohit wriggled and flung an arm toward the sky box.

The room fell silent when a large door at the side rolled up and admitted six armed people in black tactical gear, followed by Fuerte leaping into the fray and Flygirl flying to the rafters. A searchlight skimmed the crowd, and the Director's amplified voice demanded the spectators disperse. He sounded a little like Kenneth Branagh. Or maybe that's what she heard because he led the cavalry.

Flygirl, who Suzie knew as Jessica, soared over the crowd, a dark silhouette floating above the agents in tactical gear hurrying to Patricia's side. Suzie sank to her knees, shaking. Now that the UCU had arrived, she wanted to collapse from relief. She nearly jumped out of her skin when her hairbrush rang inside her Michael Kors bag.

"Suzie!" Patricia's voice rasped in the way it always did when she wore her lizard face. "Where are you?"

Suzie stood up and waved. "Look up."

Patricia shielded her eyes with one claw and looked up, then pointed. A few cameras followed her arm, trying to find what the Lizard Woman was pointing at, so Suzie stepped back into the shadows. She spoke into the phone. "Can someone come get me? I seem to have lost my shoes."

Half an hour later, Fuerte carried Suzie out to the transport van to keep her from wounding her bare feet in the glass-strewn parking lot. Patricia already stretched across the front bench seat, a bandage around her human-again arm. She sat up to make room for Suzie, then wrapped her arms around her, squeezing until Suzie grunted in protest. Patricia let her go and ran her hands over Suzie's hair and arms as if checking for damage.

"I'm all right," Suzie said. "Nothing a good night's sleep, some arnica, and a shopping expedition can't fix." She stretched her legs and wriggled her dirty feet. "The Department owes me a new pair of shoes." She considered her bloody skirt and damaged blouse. "And a new outfit."

Patricia didn't laugh. She still stared intently at Suzie, no hint of the usual reckless gleam in her eye. "If anything had happened to you…"

Suzie raised a hand. "Stop." Things could have been a lot worse. If their captors hadn't believed her weak and harmless, escape would have been even more difficult and dangerous. But none of that was Patricia's problem, even if she assumed it was. Suzie already planned to put together a hostage situation training program, and she would enroll as the first participant.

"I chose this life," she said, taking Patricia's hand. "Even before I chose you. And I wouldn't give either up." Then, she let her head fall against Patricia's shoulder and closed her eyes. They could figure the rest out tomorrow.

IV

FLYGIRL'S SECOND CHANCE

INTRODUCTION

Jessica "Flygirl" Roark has been through a lot in her thirty-two years: a knee injury that ended her potential career in gymnastics, an early and probably ill-advised marriage, and raising sons. She survived ovarian cancer, but her marriage didn't. Her first outing as a super-hero nearly got her killed.

But it hasn't been all challenges. In fact, she says that she's more herself in her new superheroic life than she has ever been before. In this story, we see her new confidence blossom and her love life take off. If you've been cheering for Walter and Jessica since they met in book two, *Change of Life*, you're going to love this story!

This story fits into the universe after book three but doesn't contain any significant spoilers for the other books.

FLYGIRL'S SECOND CHANCE

J essica lay in bed watching the ceiling fan spin. The blurred white circle made by the blades seemed to match her spinning brain, looping through all the details of her upcoming wedding. She had sworn she wouldn't become one of "those" brides, obsessing over flowers and cakes and table decorations, unable to talk of anything else and driving her friends and family crazy. But that didn't mean she didn't want it all to go perfectly. With only two more days to go, she couldn't fight the feeling she had forgotten something.

She reached for her phone on the pillow next to her and discovered she was floating six inches above the bed. Again. Her nerves must really be getting to her. She hadn't had this much trouble staying on the ground since the change first came upon her. She burped unceremoniously and plopped back down on the bed, using the spring to vault back onto her feet.

No point in lying there. The sleep train had left the station, abandoning her on the platform. She might as well go fly.

Crossing to her closet, she shoved aside her ordinary clothes and pulled out one of the garment bags in the far left. She paused to look at the larger garment bag on the far right but resisted the urge to take out her wedding gown and check it again. Examining her dress wouldn't calm her nerves like kicking some bad guy butt.

When she tossed her uniform on the bed, the body armor inserts jangled with a metallic clunk. The sound comforted her, promising safety and protection.

A few minutes later, dressed as her alter-ego, Flygirl, she examined herself in the mirror. She'd chosen the blue and white, flashier version of her uniform, her blond hair tucked under the mask with the fake red locks hanging beneath. When night flying, she nearly always wore the recognizable one so people didn't call 911 to report a burglar like they sometimes did when she went out in her all black stealth uniform. She picked up her phone and checked in, letting dispatch know about her planned extra patrol in the Moore Square area. Acknowledgement came quickly, without an assignment. Jessica tried not to feel disappointed that the city was quiet.

Stopping by the guest bedroom, where her mother had slept more often lately, she rapped lightly on the door and pushed it open when no one answered. Eva Roark had fallen asleep with her book across her chest again. Jessica laid a hand on her shoulder and shook her gently. "I'm going on patrol, Mom."

Her mother murmured, still mostly asleep, "Everything okay?"

"Yes. No call. You'll handle the boys if they wake?"

The answering agreement fell softly, so Jessica added a note to the hall chalkboard, too, just in case. "On patrol. Ask Grandma. Love you both!"

Then she climbed the narrow staircase to the attic and opened the windows. She could see the serene streets of her suburban neighborhood. At two in the morning on a weeknight, she could make out a few stars despite the light pollution caused by Springfield's growing cityscape. Leaning out, she breathed in the night air: a little moist with the lingering humidity of a Southern summer. It would feel great to fly.

With one last check to make sure no one watched, Jessica crouched against the window frame and threw herself into the sky. The moment of leaping was always a thrill.

Night air folded around her like an embrace, and when she got up to speed, the wind whipped around her head and shoulders. *Glorious.* She stretched her body and reveled in the feeling. She never felt as free as when she flew.

A few years earlier, when she struggled to control her flight and worried she would drift endlessly until she cartwheeled into the upper atmosphere, she would never have predicted that flying would bring her joy. Now, she bolted across the night sky, tucking her body to increase her speed and fought down the urge to laugh from sheer exuberance.

She didn't stop until she arrived in the main square of the downtown city park, alighting atop an ancient tree to survey the area. The branches trembled when she landed, but the homeless man sleeping on the bench near the tree pulled his silver survival blanket over his head. Hovering near the cover of the treetops, Jessica floated in a small circle, checking out the park as far as she could see. *Quiet.*

She decided to make a circuit anyway. Spiraling into the air, she directed her body toward the lake. The flat surface reflected the city lights, and she dropped to skim the surface, dipping her fingertips into the water the way a heron might dip its wings. Movement and a flash of light on the far side of the lake caught her eye, so she darted to the reeds along the west side and rose into the low branches of the bordering trees, moving stealthily toward the figures she'd seen.

There were two. A small scruffy man, lying on the ground with his arms curled over his face protectively, and looming over him, a gargantuan, reptilian brute whose green scales shimmered in the streetlights. The muscular creature's shock of red hair waved each time it moved.

When the Lizard Woman stomped her foot near his elbows, the trembling man whimpered as if he might cry. Jessica wouldn't have blamed him if he did. She clutched the trunk of her sheltering tree, imagining facing an adversary with such a frightening visage without special powers or skills. Thankfully, she wouldn't have to.

Leaping from the tree, she flew to the scene, dropping neatly behind the man on the ground. "What's going on?" she asked.

The man tried to scuttle away but bumped against her shins and rolled into a ball at her feet. Jessica looked down at him, suppressing a laugh.

"Purse-snatcher," growled the lizard beast, who shrank before Jessica's eyes into her friend Patricia's more normal, but tall, size.

The failed mugger missed the change, cowering at Jessica's feet.

Patricia shook her still-scaly head and snapped cuffs around the man's wrists before moving him to a nearby bench. Jessica picked up the bright blue clutch purse from the ground. "Did you call it in yet?"

Grunting, the Lizard Woman nodded. Good. Patricia was following procedure for once. She'd been suspended twice since they'd been recruited by the Department's Unusual Cases Unit, or UCU, both times for breaking protocol to handle things her own way. Sometimes Jessica wondered if her friend had done the right thing by joining. She might have been happier had she remained a rumor, the legendary Lizard Woman of Springfield. On her own, she'd have to adhere to fewer rules. Of course, she'd also have no backup and face the possibility of prosecution for vigilantism, so maybe this was the best outcome after all. She'd hate to have to bail her bridesmaid out of jail.

Jessica peeked inside the purse and saw a wallet and car keys, as well as a phone. The thief hadn't even had time to rummage through the contents yet. "Where's the victim?"

"Other side of the bridge."

Jessica nodded. "If you've got this, I'll let her know where we are."

"Sure thing, Flygirl. She's a tall African American woman in a dress that matches the purse. I told her to wait there."

Jessica tossed Patricia the purse. "You'd better hold onto this until the retrieval team gets here to take statements."

Patricia held it against the scaly torso of her fighting form and grinned, the expression horrifying, like watching a crocodile smile. She struck an exaggerated girly pose. "I don't think it goes with my outfit." Flipping a hand through her hair, making the short strands stand like the spikes on her shoulders, Patricia trudged over to the bench and sank down beside the would-be thief who scooted as far away as he dared.

Flying to the area where Patricia left the victim took only a moment. The purse snatcher hadn't gotten far. The woman stood right where Patricia described, flapping her arms in angry frustration while another woman with her clucked soothingly. Jessica cleared her throat while hovering in the air, silencing the women, then lowered herself gently beside them. It still gave her a rush when she got to pull a super-heroic move like that. "Is one of you missing a purse?"

The tall woman jostled her shorter friend aside. "That's me. Did the Lizard Woman catch him?"

Jessica nodded. "She's got him by the lake. If you would follow me, please?" Jessica lifted into the air with a showy gymnastic turn then floated on the gentle breeze, slowly enough that the two women could follow.

They chattered below her and seemed more excited than frightened by their experience. The shorter woman was fangirling about having seen the Lizard Woman with her very own eyes. Jessica hoped Patricia would agree to pose for a few pictures. Patricia didn't care much for the PR part of the job, but it really did help with public trust, especially for her, since she could be downright terrifying if she chose.

After the retrieval team arrived and took statements and photos, Jessica and Patricia walked off together toward the center of the park. "What are you doing up so late?" Patricia asked. "I'm usually the one looking for trouble after midnight."

"Couldn't sleep."

"Jitters?"

"Not really. I mean, I know Walter is the right man for me. But I want everything to go right, you know?"

Patricia looked around. Jessica did the same, nodding to indicate the coast was clear. Patricia transformed back into her human self, a barefoot middle-aged woman wearing a jogging outfit. Though the

Unusual Crimes Unit had developed clothing that would stretch with Patricia's transformations and hold together even if she brought out her full armor and spikes, they hadn't found any kind of shoe solution yet.

They sat under a tree together. Patricia retrieved a bag she'd left hanging from one of its branches and offered Jessica a bottle of water. Jessica wasn't thirsty, but she took it to be companionable. Patricia slid her feet back into her running shoes, and Jessica fought the urge to smooth down her friend's hair. The short red locks stuck up in sweaty spikes. The purse snatcher must have given her a decent run.

"It's going to be fine, you know," said Patricia. "As long as you end up married at the end, it's a successful ceremony. The rest is for fun. Remember that." She jabbed Jessica in the ribs, making her flinch. "You're supposed to be having fun."

Jessica nodded. "The Director is still mad I wouldn't let him use it as a publicity stunt and get married as Flygirl."

Patricia snorted. "Would that make Walter your Lois Lane?"

"Hey, he could rock a miniskirt."

Patricia covered her face. "Ow! My eyes! Damn. I can see that too well."

Jessica's mind's eye had turned her scientist-fiancé's lab coat into a trench-coat dress, his hairy legs crossed beneath while he waggled his eyebrows at her. *Too funny.* "How's your dress?" Jessica asked.

Patricia scowled at her. "I still can't believe you're making me wear a dress. I ought to transform in the middle of the ceremony to punish you for making me wear foundation garments."

"Spanx, Patricia. They're called Spanx."

"Like that's less ridiculous? That sounds kinkier than your vanilla love life is ever likely to be."

Jessica smiled. "A little vanilla might be good, you know. My life has been far too exciting lately."

"You know I've got your back." Patricia paused and drained the remainder of her water bottle before stuffing it back in the knapsack. "Suzie likes the dress. Says it makes her think of something from a black and white movie. Glamorous."

"So, should I aim my bouquet at one of you? You planning to make an honest woman of her?"

Patricia's face widened in horror. "Oh, hell no! Things are good as they are."

"Yeah." Jessica sighed. "They really are."

"You don't sound convinced."

"I feel like something is missing. But I've been over and over the plan."

"Talk to Suzie. She's great at this kind of thing."

"You sure? It might give her ideas."

"If Suzie's got ideas, I'll hear about it soon enough." Patricia looked back at the lake. The sky beyond had lightened, a dusky pink smearing like cake icing against the long thin clouds. "Come on. It's almost morning. I bet she's up."

"I'll meet you there. It's a beautiful night for flying."

Jessica took the long way around, circling the park again and sitting atop the sculpture of the giant acorn to watch the sunrise before heading to Patricia's condo. She waved at children waiting for the school bus and nearly caused a fender bender before she decided she'd better fly a bit higher. Flygirl was well known in Springfield, but seeing her defy gravity still shocked people.

The coolness was already leaving the air. It would be another hot day.

When she landed on Patricia's back deck, Suzie had laid out a bathrobe for her and pulled the privacy shades. *Considerate.* Jessica hadn't really planned on going visiting after her patrol and didn't have anything less attention-getting to wear. She pulled off her mask as she walked into the kitchen, fluffing her short, blond hair where it had bunched up and plastered to her head.

Patricia and Suzie stood near the coffeepot, holding matching white mugs of steaming coffee and chatting. Patricia wore her running clothes from the night's jaunt. Suzie wore a flowing floral skirt and a charming sweater set that emphasized her slender shoulders and tiny waist. Standing next to Patricia, she looked like a Barbie doll, or maybe Patricia's daughter. The more-than-two decades between them really showed in that moment, but they were well suited. It took a strong woman to hold her own with Patricia, and Suzie was up to the task.

Suzie noticed her first and bounced over for a hug. "Hey you! Nice flight?"

Jessica nodded and hopped up onto a kitchen stool and leaned on the counter, looking around at the small chrome and glass kitchen. Her own house had a giant kitchen that would inspire the envy of a great cook. Since she didn't actually cook, it seemed like a waste. Something simple and sleek like this would be much more appropriate.

Suzie handed her a mug of coffee already doctored with just the right amount of cream. "I hear you might have forgotten something."

Jessica nodded. She liked Suzie, but realizing Patricia and Suzie talked about her weirded her out a bit. Couples do that, of course, talk about their mutual friends. Imagining the normally taciturn Patricia and bubbly Suzie hashing out how to help left Jessica feeling strange. Patricia had always said other people's problems were just that: other people's problems. Sharing a life with Suzie seemed to be softening her stance. They weren't the likeliest of couples, but they worked well together. Even Leonel said Patricia was a better person with Suzie in her life.

Suzie hopped onto the other high stool, shoving Jessica's Flygirl mask to the side to make room for her coffee mug. The women were nearly the same size, at five-foot-nothing and just over a hundred pounds. Their feet dangled, and they both had to scoot forward to rest their shoes on the intended support. "Tell me about the ceremony, step by step." Suzie turned and fluttered a hand at Patricia. "Go, shower and take a nap. We're talking girl stuff here."

Patricia arched an eyebrow, but obeyed, leaving the two younger women alone. At first Jessica felt silly, but Suzie's enthusiasm soon won her over and had her gushing about the Asiatic lilies for her bouquet and the tiny beakers in the table settings for coffee creamer. "Definitely no tea!" she added, and Suzie laughed behind her hand. Tea had been, in part, responsible for Jessica's flying ability, and Jessica had not been able to make herself drink it since her change.

When the two had talked through the whole plan, from morning hair and makeup appointments through leaving for the honeymoon, Suzie leaned back in her chair and stretched her feet against the counter, her bright blue slides gently tapping the tile front. She clicked her shoes a few more times, then slid off the stool and paced around the living room.

Jessica spun her stool to watch, finishing her third cup of coffee and nibbling on a muffin she'd snagged from a platter on the counter. When Suzie mulled something over, she walked in tight figure-eights, a precision pattern that bent around on itself over and over again while she pulled her hair up and let it fall. It was best not to interrupt her rhythm.

Suddenly Suzie stopped and turned back to Jessica. "Tell me about your first wedding."

Jessica nearly choked on her coffee. Spluttering, she set the cup on the counter. "What?"

"When you married the boys' father. What's his name?"

"Nathan."

"Yes. Nathan. What was the wedding like?"

"We didn't have one."

Suzie raised an eyebrow. "Just a paper signing?"

"Pretty much. He picked me up from my college dorm and drove us to City Hall."

"What did your parents think?"

"My mom supported me. Even when I'm being stupid, my mom always supports me."

"And your dad?"

Jessica shook her head, surprised to feel tears welling. "He said Nathan wasn't good enough for me and the lack of a wedding proved it." Jessica slid off the stool and went to the sink to rinse her fingers. Drying them on a towel, she turned. "He died not long after that. He never got to find out he was right about Nathan. And he never got to meet Walter."

The two women remained silent for a long moment, then Suzie spoke, her voice soft and full of kindness. "I think that's what you've forgotten. Walter is a great guy, and I bet your dad would have liked him. He would have walked you down the aisle proudly, knowing you found a partner who will help you make something of yourself and your life instead of using you as some kind of battery to fuel himself without ever recharging you in return."

Jessica flushed bright red and bunched the towel in her fingers. Anger rose in her, burning under her skin. She wanted to throw the towel at Suzie. What could she possibly know about it? Suzie was practically a child herself, not even thirty yet. She still had both her parents. She'd never even been married. Nathan hadn't been a great husband, but it hadn't been like that.

Had it?

Abruptly, the anger dropped out from under her, silenced by the realization that the girl was right. Jessica slumped against the sink and took in a ragged breath, full of unshed tears.

"I thought Patricia was the straight-talking one." Jessica wiped at her eyes with the back of her hand, feeling sheepish and wondering if she owed Suzie an apology.

Suzie smiled. "There's a reason she loves me, and it's not just because I'm cute. I'm also completely amazing."

"Yes, you are." The voice came from the doorway where Patricia stood dressed in a fluffy bathrobe, wrapping her hair into a turban. Suzie clicked across the hardwood floor and offered her cheek for a kiss.

"I've got to get to work. You want a ride, Jessica, or are you flying in?"

Jessica checked the clock. Seven-fifteen. "If I leave now, I can catch my boys before they leave for school." She slid the robe off and hung it across the back of the barstool chair.

Suzie handed her Flygirl's mask and waited while Jessica pulled it over her head, helping her tuck her blond hair beneath before offering her a quick hug. "We'll find a way to include your dad in your special day. Give me a little while to think about it."

"Thanks." Jessica didn't dare say more, not wanting emotion to take over again. She went out onto the balcony and crouched on the railing, turning to wave before she leapt into the brightening sky.

The rest of the morning zipped by in a blur. After seeing her boys off to school, she'd driven to headquarters as the seemingly ordinary Jessica Roark and worked through the security checkpoints under the bank that served as a front for the Unusual Cases Unit. She had barely finished submitting her paperwork on the purse-snatcher when they got called to provide backup at an accident across town.

The accident involved an overturned semi-truck on the loop around Springfield and several wrecked cars in the vicinity. Traffic accidents didn't usually merit a UCU call, but the truck dangled over an overpass bridge, in danger of dropping to the layer below, so the entire area had become unstable. Normal safety and rescue workers couldn't access parts of the scene. Heavy trucks and equipment would only further destabilize the structure.

Because Flygirl didn't have to touch the ground, she flew reconnaissance, looking for anyone trapped or injured. Flashing lights reflected strangely in the dust and smoke, forcing her to search in short bursts. Following an imaginary grid to make sure she didn't miss anything, she peered into windows of the scattered cars parked on the bridge and inside the precariously balanced truck, but it appeared all the people had evacuated safely. Her heart slowed down. If the workers under the bridge got the cars cleared out, they could avoid human casualties, even if the worst happened and the truck fell to the road below.

She had just turned back when she spotted it. Beyond the truck, a small, bright blue car had been trapped between the truck and the crumbling railing. No one could have seen it without getting close.

The driver's side of the car was jammed up against the cracked retaining wall, trapping its occupants. The truck's overturned trailer blocked the view from nearly all angles.

The woman behind the wheel appeared unconscious while the man in the passenger seat struggled against the deployed airbag and tried to calm the two children in the back, one strapped into a car seat and the other maybe six or seven years old, no longer buckled into her booster. Both children sobbed loud, howling tears. Flygirl flew around the car, examining it from every angle. The damaged passenger doors couldn't be opened, but the occupants had escaped crushing themselves. She couldn't get these people out of the car, not without power tools.

She rested a hand on the glass as she hovered, stunning the children into silence. "Help is on the way!" she shouted. She smiled broadly and saluted before she jetted back to the other side of the overpass where emergency vehicles waited, explaining the situation over her headset as she flew.

A team surrounded Fuerte, already strapping him into safety tethering when she arrived. Leonel "Fuerte" Alvarez, Jessica's best friend and man of honor, looked every inch a superhero in his golden sun mask and body-hugging black pants. The two had first met while dealing with the changes Dr. Liu had wrought in their lives, changes that gave Jessica flight and transformed the Latina grandmother into a man with super-strength. Their friendship had only grown stronger as they worked together at the UCU.

All of them froze when a loud metallic groan washed over the scene. A man in a blue jumpsuit, an agent Jessica didn't recognize, ran up and yelled at everyone to hurry—the truck had shifted, and the structure couldn't take the weight.

"There are children in that car," Flygirl said and gripped Fuerte's hand. The two of them took off, Fuerte running along the most stable path while Flygirl rushed ahead through the air. More than once, Fuerte had to leap over holes as he ran.

Flygirl got to the car first and peered in through the glass. The man in the passenger seat who had been struggling against the airbag earlier now lay back in his seat, maybe unconscious. Just unconscious, she hoped. The older child in the backseat peered back at Flygirl, holding the crying toddler in her lap, her expression vacant. Flygirl worried the girl might be in shock—she barely seemed to notice the little boy squirming in her arms. Her skinny chest lifted and fell quickly, suggesting hyperventilation. Between the glare of sunlight and the dirt on the glass, Jessica couldn't be sure about the girl's pallor or dilation of her pupils, but she clearly needed medical attention.

"Flygirl!" The voice in her earpiece startled her, and she spun around to track Fuerte's progress. He gave instructions as he picked his way across the treacherous bridge. She flew to the far side of the bridge and took sturdy cables from the crane operator, arriving back at the car just as Fuerte ran up. Flygirl hurried to attach the rappelling cables to his harness, then floated out of the way to let him work.

Fuerte grabbed the back passenger-side door at a dented corner and peeled it back like the lid of a tuna can, sliding it across the pavement gently, careful of the crumbling concrete. It sparked as it slid. "Get the kids!" he shouted.

Flygirl swooped in, pulling out the limp, unresisting girl and the struggling, wailing toddler, then tucked them into her arms and spiraled into the air, a move that would have made her own boys gasp with joy and tighten their arms around her neck.

The toddler went wide-eyed and mercifully silent, but the little girl slumped listlessly in her arms. Flygirl didn't watch Fuerte work, but headed for the nearest ambulance, putting on a burst of speed strong enough to make her cheeks ripple with the wind. Flying with the children in her arms knocked her off balance, but Flygirl didn't let that stop her. Those upper body workouts would prove their worth today.

After handing off the children to the EMTs, she vaulted back into the air and returned to the scene. For more room to maneuver, Fuerte had nudged the cab of the truck away from the trapped car with the unconscious parents inside. Flygirl hovered in the air above the scene, keeping an eye on Fuerte's safety cables, ready to leap in if they tangled or snared. The bridge groaned ominously, and Flygirl tensed at the sound. The sirens and lights dropped below her awareness as she hung in the sky, taut and focused on her partner.

Fuerte swung his body around the car with a delicacy of movement surprising in a man his size. He grabbed the chassis from the front, lifting the front two wheels off the ground. Flygirl held her breath, praying the structure would remain stable long enough to free the car as Fuerte stalked backward, tugging the vehicle slowly away from the edge where it perched.

When he made enough room, Fuerte ducked behind the car and shoved. It seemed to take no more effort than pushing a stroller. Flygirl darted forward and reached into the driver's side past the broken glass to grab the steering wheel over the fluttering, deflated airbag. She flew alongside the car and steered as Fuerte pushed from behind.

The couple of times she dared to look back, clouds of concrete dust almost entirely obscured Fuerte, but she caught reassuring glimpses of his sunshine-yellow mask. The car had just nosed onto the road on the other side of the overpass bridge when Fuerte dropped out of view.

Rescue workers scrambled to attend to the parents strapped into the car, but Flygirl vaulted over them, shouting. "Fuerte!" Her heart in her throat, she peered into the hole where Fuerte had disappeared.

He hung there, suspended by his rappelling gear, kicking his feet and rocking but unable to reach anything helpful. He grinned up at her. "Little help?"

Touching down, Flygirl squatted and stretched out an arm to tow him nearer the edge of the pavement. The six-foot tall strongman was far too heavy for her to pull out, but if she could get him a handhold, he and the crane operator would manage the rest. If not for the safety gear, Fuerte would have fallen through the bridge and onto the road below.

After he tugged himself back up onto the pavement, the two sat panting for a moment. Fuerte grinned and patted Flygirl's knee. "Shouldn't you be working on your wedding vows?"

"You don't have to practice when you're speaking from the heart."

"Are you nervous? Can I help with anything?"

Jessica squinted into the sun. She thought again about what Suzie said. The thing missing from the ceremony wasn't a what, but a who: her father. Leonel couldn't fix that. No one could. But she felt lucky to have a friend who wanted to help.

She had reached out to squeeze his hand, when the entire structure shook again. Fuerte gripped his safety gear to avoid falling back through the hole in the pavement, and Flygirl lifted into the air, spinning to take in the scene. Her earpiece exploded with chatter, too much to understand. She clicked it off.

Fuerte, on his feet now, stood below her and scanned the scene. People in UCU blue jumpsuits ran alongside firefighters and police officers. Blue and red flashing lights reflected off the emergency vehicles on both sides of the bridge. Flygirl took it all in as seconds ticked by. Clicking her headset back on and flicking to a private channel for the UCU team, she reported what she could see. There had to be a way to stop the truck from falling and completely destroying the bridge and the road below.

When orders came, Flygirl left Fuerte to make his own way back to the overturned truck and flew to the UCU van to collect a thick support cable attached to a giant winch. Three civilian wreckers parked alongside the military van.

Flygirl let the cable play out between her gloved hands as she flew. Behind her, more agents in UCU blue jumpsuits set up supports and hooked the cable through them. Ignoring the shouts and sirens and the lights and clouds of raised dust, she narrowed her focus to her part in the plan, trusting the team to make sure it came together.

Back at the crumbling barrier, the truck shifted again. More of the trailer now hung over the edge, threatening anew to overbalance and topple the entire vehicle as well as chunks of the bridge onto the roadway below. Worries about people below and whether the police had cleared the scene flashed across Flygirl's mind in too-vivid detail, forcing her to clamp down on her imagination before it derailed her ability to help.

Flygirl flew back and forth between the winches and the overturned truck at top speed, affixing cables to the truck so they could pull it back from the edge.

Meanwhile, Fuerte gripped the cab of the truck, preventing further slippage while she and the other agents worked. The sun glinted off the taut silver lines tethering the broken trailer to the wreckers.

It wasn't enough. Even with the crane and cabling to support him, Fuerte struggled to keep his footing and fight the pull of gravity of the 18,000 pounds of metal.

Thinking fast, Flygirl dove toward the gap where the cab and trailer hitched together. "On your left," she called to Fuerte. He didn't answer aloud, but leaned right, widening the gap and giving her as much room to work as he could without losing his grip. Twisting her body, Flygirl slid into the narrow space, affixing the hook end of her cable and jetting back out the other side. Hovering above the wreck, she signaled the team to tighten the slack.

As the final cable tightened, Fuerte slowly released his hold and moved aside. The bridge groaned, and Fuerte prayed in Spanish. Although she understood few of the words, Flygirl found the ritual and rhythm comforting. The two heroes watched together, ready to jump back in if the plan failed. Flygirl sucked in a breath and held it, releasing it only when the cable straightened and held. Relieved chatter spilled out of the headset.

And then, one of the cables snapped.

The anchor point had failed, the weight too much. The high whine of the winches became a screech, and an electrical stench bloomed in the air. Curses abounded on the radio link.

All around them, chaos erupted. Voices shouted and sparks flew. A chunk of the barrier, where the little blue car had been pinned, cracked and fell.

Flygirl dove and caught a section of the cable, but it jerked out of her gloved hands and flapped along the pavement. She spun in the air, disoriented. Fuerte's support crew had pulled back on his rigging, and he dangled in the air. Jessica tried not to imagine a crushed car below them.

The other cables held, but without the last one, the heaviest part of the truck resisted the pull of all the others. Taking aim, she vaulted again toward the rogue cable. The thick wire flopped around like fish on the shore. Each time she caught it, it tugged free again. Flygirl wasn't strong enough to hold it.

Fuerte dropped onto the pavement beside her, lowered there by crane. The next time she caught the cable, his black-gloved hands joined hers and held. Moving together, they untangled the cable with the practice of partners used to reading each other's intentions. Fuerte wrapped the steel cable around his arm, rolling it like an errant extension cord.

When he handed her the roll and squatted to grip the cab again, she flew around, wrapping the damaged vehicle in loops of cable like a shiny ribbon on a gift. After three times around, she returned the cable to Fuerte. As he pulled, the cable grew taut again and dragged the truck across the pavement. Fuerte turned and trudged forward, the cable over his shoulder, leaning as if walking into a heavy wind. His muscles bulged, and he cried out from the strain, but still, he pulled the cab several feet nearer the center of the bridge.

When he could go no farther, he fell to his knees.

Flygirl bolted over and took the rolled cable from him, threading it through the supports, and then ferried it to the final winch and the blue jumpsuited agent waiting to reel it in. The agent threaded it quickly and turned on the crank. They all held their breath. The makeshift safety net pulled the truck across the remains of the bridge with a metallic screech.

Flygirl alighted on the roof of the UCU van and accepted the water bottle someone tossed her, downing it while she searched the scene for Fuerte. The water tasted of sulfur, or maybe the inside of her mouth did. At last she spotted him, sitting on the ground next to an ambulance, waving off EMTs and blue jumpsuits and pouring water over his dusty face and chest—not hurt, then.

She sat atop the van, catching her breath and watching the scene. Ambulances left and tow trucks arrived. Construction cranes set up to stabilize the bridge while police redirected traffic. It would take months to repair the damage, but it could have been a lot worse.

Her earpiece buzzed against the roof of the van. She picked it up and put it back in place. "You up to talk to the news crew?"

She agreed and met Fuerte at the far end of the scene for what they had come to call "the dog and pony show." Flygirl didn't know if she was the dog or the pony, but maintaining public goodwill made the work easier for all of them.

"That was some amazing work, Flygirl."

"Thank you, Jeffrey," Jessica answered, her tone neutral. She hadn't forgotten the reporter's colorful commentary about the way her costume fit when announcing the UCU to the public. Even if he hadn't gotten lascivious on-air, he would still be her least favorite of the television reporters. Something about him set off warning signals in her brain. But it wouldn't do to insult the man while he worked, nor to lose a positive publicity opportunity, so she glued her smile in place and redirected his attention. "My colleague, Fuerte, did all the heavy lifting."

Picking up on his cue, Leonel knelt and flexed for the camera. Her friend could ham it up when the occasion called for it, which surprised Jessica given how shy he could be about such attention in private. But she appreciated his willingness to clown for the camera. It gave her a moment to focus her thoughts and review the talking points the PR department relayed to her headset. *Emphasize teamwork.* No surprise. There had been some grumbling at city council meetings about the public giving undue credit to flashy heroes.

"Seriously though, the Unusual Crimes Unit is just one part of the team of rescue workers here in Springfield." Jessica waved over one of the firefighters who had worked the winches, a young woman with bright blond hair streaked with soot. "The brave men and women of our police and rescue services had already secured the area. By the time we got here, they had the situation well in hand."

"Well, mostly in hand." The firefighter laughed, rubbing a gloved hand across her lightly freckled cheek and leaving a black smudge. "I'm glad I didn't have to catch a semi."

Fuerte clapped a hand on the woman's shoulder. "And I'm glad you kept me from falling through the holes!"

The young girl that had been trapped in the car hurtled across the pavement, a police officer chasing her, struggling to keep the squirming toddler in his arms. The child flung herself at Jessica's legs. "Flygirl!"

Disentangling the girl's fingers, Jessica knelt, doing her best to ignore the camera flashes around them and focus on the child. Tears streaked the girl's round face, and she had something sticky in her hair. "Hello, brave girl! I saw what you did back there, keeping your brother calm. He's so lucky to have you!"

The girl looked at her shoes, and Jessica tucked a finger under her chin. "Hey, now. I mean it. Staying calm and helping him feel safe was the best thing you could have done." She gave the girl a hug. "Did they take your mom and dad to the hospital?"

The child nodded against Jessica's shoulder. "Then you'd better let this nice police officer get you cleaned up so you'll be ready to see them." She placed the girl's hand in the officer's and waved good-bye.

When they waved off the reporters, Jessica spoke into her headset, asking the Department to arrange for a hospital visit for the injured couple and to find out if they needed any resources. As the two heroes walked back to catch a ride, Fuerte pulled out his phone. "¡Caray!"

"What?"

"It's four o'clock already."

The rehearsal dinner. She only had two hours to prepare. "I'll meet you there." Flygirl took to the air.

One hour later, clean and no longer smelling of smoke and oil, Jessica came downstairs to find her mother posing her sons for pictures. Frankie and Max wore navy blue suit jackets with khaki pants and sported fresh haircuts that left them both looking startled. She whistled as she walked into the room. "Who are these handsome young men?"

"Mommy!" Max plowed into her knees, and Jessica knelt to pull her younger son into her arms. She reached out a hand to her more reticent older boy, settling for stroking his arm when he didn't bend for a hug. *Already such a little man at eight years old.*

"You guys look wonderful!"

Frankie pulled at his shirt collar but smiled at the compliment. Jessica stood and looked at her family: her mother and her boys. Everyone but Walter.

Almost as if she'd read her mind, Jessica's mother piped up. "Walter is meeting us there. He had something to pick up on the way."

Driving her minivan to the restaurant, Jessica thought about the way her life had changed. Was it really only three years ago that all this had begun? Three years ago, she'd been moping on the sofa, mourning the loss of her ovaries to cancer, watching weepy movies, and sipping tea. And now she had a new career, new abilities, new friends, and a second chance at love. It had been a bumpy road to get to this place, but it was a good place to be.

The parking lot at Anna Maria's never sat empty, but they had rented the entire restaurant for the event, so only a dozen or so cars filled the spaces. The pizza and pasta place had become special to Jessica and Walter—the place they had taken their first "family dates" and where they celebrated small accomplishments in the boys' lives or when no one wanted to cook. Walter's parents hadn't been sure a pizza joint was appropriate for a rehearsal dinner, but Walter convinced them by arranging a special catered menu including pizza for the kids and fancier pasta for the adults.

The place looked lovely lit by candlelight. The tables had been moved together to form a larger group area in the center. Jessica and Walter chose to keep the party small, but they still numbered twenty. Frankie and Max ran over to join Walter's nieces and nephew at the old-fashioned juke box. The kids, granted free reign along with a small bucket of quarters, jockeyed for position to read the options and push the buttons.

"There's my girl!" Walter broke away from his mother and pulled Jessica into a hug, then leaned back to look into her eyes. "I missed you today."

"It was a busy one."

"I heard! You'll have to give me details later. Come say hi to Mom and Dad."

During the next few minutes, Jessica hugged more people than in the past three months combined. She noted happily that David had come with Leonel. The couple had been going through a rough patch as David came to terms with Leonel's new, more dangerous career with the UCU. Suzie squealed over Jessica's dress and whispered congratulations on the afternoon's work when she leaned in for her hug.

It was the first time she'd seen the whole group together, and butterflies fluttered in her stomach. Her friends were unconventional in more than one way, and she wanted this to go well. Walter's family had been welcoming, especially his mother, Sarah, but she'd gotten the impression that Walter's choice surprised many of his relatives, and she didn't want to drive any wedges between Walter and the others who loved him. Patricia handed her a soda and looked point-edly at the ground. Jessica took a sip, burped, and lowered herself back to the floor.

She'd have to be more careful. So far as Walter's family knew, he worked as a research scientist, and she was an investment banker, the cover story did explain her last-minute unavailability and strange hours. They could always claim meetings or travel for business. Jessica sometimes wished they'd come up with something flashier, so she didn't have to fake an interest in financial news all the time. Too late now, though. The story was set.

Walter's youngest niece waddled by, gripping Jessica's knee with a damp hand as she did. Jessica knelt and picked up the child. "Hey there, starshine!" Zoe's eyes went wide, and she popped her fingers back into her mouth.

Spotting them, Zoe's mother, Francine, got up from her chair and came over. "Say hi, Zoe. Say hi to Auntie Jessica." Zoe waggled her damp fingers, then grunted and tugged to be put down. Jessica acquiesced, and the two women watched her wander back to her siblings and soon-to-be cousins drawing on the paper covering the kids' table.

"Such a sweetie," Jessica said. "I miss the chubby knees and shy smiles stage sometimes." She gestured at her own boys. Frankie loomed taller than all the other children by a head, and Max could have been a darker twin to Zoe's big brother. The boys giggled, and both women smiled to hear it. Her sons already enjoyed having cousins.

"Your boys are charmers. Think you and Walter will have any more?"

Jessica blanched. "Um, no." The other woman looked uncomfortable, and Jessica rushed to explain. "It's that...I can't. I'm a survivor, you see."

She still looked confused.

Jessica felt the heat rising in her face, then Walter appeared at her elbow. "You remember, Francine. I told you. Jessica had ovarian cancer, back before I knew her."

Francine blushed. She reached out and squeezed Jessica's shoulder. "I'm so sorry. How awful of me! I hadn't realized..."

Walter put his arm around Jessica and pulled her against his side. "I'm a lucky man. I get to be a dad without having to go through pregnancy. I remember what you were like, Francine. Your husband deserves some kind of award for putting up with you."

Francine punched her brother's shoulder and wandered off to check on her children, flashing Jessica one last apologetic smile.

Walter leaned in and kissed Jessica's cheek. "You okay?"

"Yeah." Jessica sighed. "Are you?"

"Me?" Walter looked into her face, puzzled.

"You know...with the no more kids thing?"

"You kidding? I can barely keep up with you three as it is."

Jessica tilted her head, unconvinced. She would have liked to have more kids. In fact, when she'd gotten her diagnosis, she'd been hoping the doctor would tell her she was pregnant with a daughter. Instead, he had dashed those hopes forever. Was she being fair to Walter? If he married her, he'd never father any biological children.

"Hey." Walter ran a thumb over her cheek. "I mean it. I've got everything I need right here."

Just then, Walter's father stood, tapping a spoon against his glass. The room grew quiet as all attention turned to him. Walter's father, like his son, was not a tall man. He didn't share Walter's athletic nature, though, and his paunch made him appear much shorter. "Thank you all for coming tonight. Eva, Sarah, and I are so pleased to welcome you tonight. Our son has made such a fine match. Not only is Jessica an intelligent, capable, and beautiful woman, she also came with instant grandchildren!"

The room erupted in laughter, and Frankie and Max beamed. "To the bride and groom!" After everyone drank, the wait staff appeared with serving trays, and everyone tucked in for the meal.

The party continued, and Jessica's cheeks ached from smiling as the evening wound down. Walter's family dwarfed hers, and Jessica marveled at what a family meal could be like with so many people. Never a dull moment. As they all considered their dessert options, Jessica noticed Suzie setting up a projector in the corner of the room. She groaned, anticipating a slideshow of embarrassing childhood photographs.

She hadn't realized getting married would bring so many small humiliations and strange rituals into her life: the wedding showers, bachelor and bachelorette parties, registering for gifts. As the only child of two only children, Jessica hadn't grown up with aunts and uncles and cousins and had never experienced these kinds of things. She'd been too busy jet-setting with her first husband to be a part of her college friends' weddings and had married Nathan without ceremony, missing out on all the hubbub. One of the roles that came along with the title of bride apparently included "comic relief."

Jessica gasped when the projector lit up. Her father's face filled the screen. His tanned cheeks glowed as he squinted into the sun on a dock somewhere. The water behind him sparkled a vibrant green, so

Jessica thought he might have been in the Bahamas. He used to take two trips a year for scuba diving. In fact, he'd been on the way back from a diving trip in Australia when he'd suffered the heart attack that killed him. But Jessica couldn't recall ever seeing this footage before.

Eva sat beside her daughter; Walter's sister had quietly vacated the seat. Her smile might have been a little tight, but also tender and pleased. Jessica linked her fingers with her mother's and pulled them into her lap, grasping Walter's arm with her other hand. He rested his hand atop hers, patting her fingers.

Suzie pressed a button and the video played. Wind whipped her father's hair as he spoke. "Did I tell you about my Jessica? She's in a big gymnastics tournament this weekend in D.C. Her mother's taking her." He paused, looking into the camera, and Jessica felt as if he looked straight at her. She had nearly forgotten the sound of his voice after all these years, but hearing him, it came rushing back. "I hate to miss it. My girl, she's something else. You should see her, Mick. She's amazing. So talented, so strong. So smart. I'm so proud of her. Dang, but my girl can fly!"

A song began to play. Something sweet about how "everybody's looking for that something." But Jessica didn't hear it. Nor did she see the childhood pictures of herself and Walter, though the *oohs* and *ahs* of the group testified to the charm of the choices that had been made. Her eyes were damp and her vision blurred, but her heart soared.

Suzie had done it. She'd found a way to bring her father to her wedding. Jessica didn't need superpowers to fly. She'd get there on love alone.

ACKNOWLEDGEMENTS

I'm grateful for all the generous friends, colleagues, and readers who supported me in getting this far. I hope we can continue to enjoy this ride together.

ABOUT THE AUTHOR

Samantha Bryant teaches Spanish to middle schoolers. Clearly, she's tougher than she looks. She writes *The Menopausal Superhero* series of novels and other feminist-leaning speculative fiction. When she's not writing or teaching, Samantha enjoys family time, watching old movies, baking, reading, gaming, walking in the woods with her rescue dog, and going places. Her favorite gift is tickets (to just about anything). You can find her on Twitter and Instagram @samanthab-writer or at: http://samanthabryant.com

ALSO BY SAMANTHA BRYANT

Menopausal Superheroes

Going Through the Change

Change of Life

Face the Change

FRIENDS OF FALSTAFF

Thank You to All our Falstaff Books Patrons, who get extra digital content each month! To be featured here and see what other great rewards we offer, go to www.patreon.com/falstaffbooks.

PATRONS

Dino Hicks
John Hooks
John Kilgallon
Larissa Lichty
Travis & Casey Schilling
Staci-Leigh Santore
Sheryl R. Hayes
Scott Norris
Samuel Montgomery-Blinn
Junkle

www.ingramcontent.com/pod-product-compliance
Lightning Source LLC
Chambersburg PA
CBHW050255110726
47898CB00007B/2418